S...
CH...CE

BY

JOSIE METCALFE

MILLS & BOON®

All the characters in this book have no existence outside the imagination of the author, and have no relation whatsoever to anyone bearing the same name or names. They are not even distantly inspired by any individual known or unknown to the author, and all the incidents are pure invention.

*First published in Great Britain 1997
Harlequin Mills & Boon Limited,
Eton House, 18-24 Paradise Road, Richmond, Surrey TW9 1SR*

© Josie Metcalfe 1997

ISBN 0 263 80441 0

*Set in Times 10 on 12 pt. by
Rowland Phototypesetting Limited
Bury St Edmunds, Suffolk*

03-9711-46652-D

*Printed and bound in Great Britain
by Mackays of Chatham PLC, Chatham*

CHAPTER ONE

'No way!' The deep husky voice was outraged. 'I won't do it, Leo. . .not even for you!'

'But, Wolff. . .' Leo began in his most persuasive tone.

'No!' his old friend reiterated firmly. 'This is the sort of stunt we might have pulled when we were students, but now. . .!'

'Please, Wolff. I'm desperate.' Leo ran the fingers of both hands through his hair as he paced agitatedly backwards and forwards, leaving the thick blond strands standing up in tufts all over his head while he navigated through the scattered piles of Wolff's belongings. 'The bloke I hired to do it had his appendix out this morning and I only got the message an hour ago.'

'So?' He fixed Leo with an impassive stare, knowing that his ice-blue eyes could intimidate most people with their laser-like intensity.

'So the Autumn Ball starts in less than three hours and I've lost my star prize!'

'There are plenty of other prizes,' Wolff rebutted calmly as he finally allowed himself to relax against the high-backed leather comfort of Leo's favourite fireside chair, stretching his long legs out and frowning absently at the rumpled state of the elderly jeans he'd managed to unearth from the muddle.

He folded his arms across the lean plane of his stomach, the rolled-up sleeves of his shirt very white against the deep tan of his skin as he subsided into quiescence.

Wolff's very stillness was in striking contrast to the anxious activity of his long-time friend as he returned to his objections. 'You've just spent most of the afternoon telling me that you've had some fabulous prizes donated, and the way you're going to be presenting even the lesser ones sounds as if there'll be plenty of prizes to go round.'

'Not like *this* one!' Leo protested urgently. '*This* prize is the one that's sold the tickets. . .'

'Oh, come on. . .!' Wolff shook his head chidingly and when he felt the drag of his over-long dark hair against the butter-soft upholstery he remembered with a twist of distaste that, apart from a shower and change of clothes, he still hadn't had time to do anything about his unkempt appearance.

The unexpected change in plans meant that this was just one more thing to think about before he was due to start work tomorrow. He really needed the rest of today to get himself organised. It was good of Leo to put him up until he could find his own place, but. . .

'No, really! I'm serious!' Leo pushed a pile of journals aside and perched himself on the edge of his sturdy coffee-table, then leant forward to press his case.

'I'll admit that there was the usual loyal interest in the Autumn Ball from the senior members of staff, but even with the added attraction of the auction they can't come up with the sort of money we need to finance the scanner appeal without help. To make a success of it, we needed to get the *whole* of the hospital interested.'

Wolff nodded his understanding. He'd just spent endless months trying to work out how to make pennies stretch as far as pounds, and had then watched the tragic results when it didn't—*couldn't*—work.

Openly encouraged by his friend's apparent attention, Leo continued.

'It was Polly's idea to make the whole proceedings more light-hearted—she suggested having the ticket draw—and as soon as the word got out we could hardly sell tickets fast enough! Against all expectations, we've actually got a chance of making our target by the end of the night. We should have the scanner months ahead of schedule!'

'That's fantastic,' Wolff said sincerely. 'But what I don't understand is why you ever thought of *that*!' He gestured with one lean hand towards the costume, hanging behind the door. 'Where's the *rest* of it, for heaven's sake?'

Leo's golden eyes gleamed wickedly. 'The costume was delivered just before I got the message about the appendectomy, and I can only presume that the dancer supplies the rest of it—his body!'

'But. . .' Wolf began faintly when he realised exactly how few garments the hanger contained. Even if he'd been tempted to take the job on for bravado, the thought of exposing *that* much of himself to public gaze was enough to paralyse him with stage fright. It was a good job he had no intention of. . .

'Oh, come on, Wolff! You're the only one I know who could pull it off. I'd do it myself if I wasn't going to be fully occupied as auctioneer. Anyway, you've always been a far better dancer than I am, and the rest of your equipment isn't bad. . .!'

Wolff felt a wash of heat travel along his cheek-bones at the assessing glance his friend threw his outstretched body, and thanked his lucky stars that the deep tan he'd

developed—in spite of his avoidance of the fierce sun—
would hide the fact from his irreverent friend. He'd never
hear the last of it if Leo realised how easily embarrassed
he still was. . .

'Leo, I *can't*,' he began, marshalling his thoughts to kill
the idea off once and for all. 'I'm absolutely shattered after
all that travelling—I was supposed to have nearly ten days
to get myself together before I started here, remember?'

'Your part will only take half an hour, and then you can
come back here and crash out,' Leo wheedled. 'And the
short notice is hardly *my* fault, anyway. How was I to
know that Nick would take it into his head to ask you to
start early so that he and Polly could get married
straight away?'

'Huh!' Wolff scoffed. 'By your own admission, you've
been scheming to push the two of them together for weeks.'

'Yes, but. . .'

'Anyway,' Wolff continued, determined to finish his
objections with the final clincher, 'I'm supposed to be
covering the department for Nick while he's away. What
sort of authority will I be able to wield if the whole hospital
knows I've taken part in this sort of stunt? You haven't
even got any control over who I'd have to dance with—
it could be anyone from one of the most junior nurses to
the wife of one of the senior consultants!'

Leo was silent for a moment, then a crafty expression
crept over his face.

'Not necessarily,' he murmured, half under his breath,
as he gazed almost absent-mindedly across the room. 'In
fact, that's the beauty of this outfit, old friend,' Leo crowed
triumphantly as he leapt to his feet again and clambered

exuberantly across his cluttered living room to reach for the despised costume.

'Look!' He held up a black satin domino mask. 'Your hair's still all long and shaggy and you'll have this on your face. By the time you come on duty tomorrow you'll have had a shave and a haircut, and no one will ever know that it was you!'

'*I'll* know,' Wolff muttered darkly, but he had a nasty feeling that he might just as well give in now as prolong the agony. He'd known Leo since they'd met during their training rotation under Nick Prince, and knew that he was as tenacious as a terrier when he got his teeth into an idea.

'But you'll do it,' Leo said hopefully, obviously scenting victory.

'Under duress,' he conceded, a sinking sensation taking up residence in his gut as he became more and more certain that he was making a monumental mistake.

'But I'll tell you now that I'm going to be wearing more than half a handkerchief to cover my essentials and, while I'm up there making a complete ass of myself, I'm going to be concentrating on the fact that you'll owe me—big time! Now, tell me what I've got to do before I come to my senses. . .'

'Oh-h, let me sit down,' Laura groaned as she flopped onto the seat beside Hannah. 'My feet are killing me!'

'And we're hardly halfway through the shift,' her friend pointed out.

'Don't remind me.' Laura scowled as she leaned her head back against the upholstery. 'The whole morning has been filled with a succession of my least favourite cases— they seem to be the same whichever hospital you work at.'

'You mean the patients who should have made an appointment to see their doctors, but decided to come here instead because they thought they'd be seen faster?'

'And then they create hell because triage means that the more urgent cases are taken through ahead of them and they're going to be late for work?'

'Exactly! How many have you had today?'

'So far, only one—a businessman who was certain he had an ulcer, and wanted some medicine to take straight away so that he could enjoy his usual boozy power-lunch at twelve o'clock.'

'Was that the one who thought he was more important than the little boy who'd cut his leg open on broken glass?'

Laura nodded. 'That's the one—a real sweetheart he was.'

'I bet he was delighted when Leo told him to go back to his doctor if he wanted to be referred to a specialist,' Hannah commented with an almost gleeful expression, knowing that the hospital was committed to educating the patients as to the *real* purpose of an accident and emergency department.

'Especially when he suggested that the man could do with losing at least fifty pounds in weight and drinking milk instead of martinis!'

They both laughed wryly.

'Well, as far as I can see, the patients are turning up in droves today on purpose,' Hannah said, returning to her original complaint. 'They must know we're going to the Ball tonight and want us to be too tired to enjoy ourselves.'

'We?' Laura demanded, picking out the one word which jarred on her sensitive antennae. 'Which "we" are you talking about?'

'You and me, of course,' Hannah elaborated as she finally gave in and copied Laura, sliding her feet out of her shoes and wriggling her toes blissfully.

'Me? I'm not going,' Laura said in surprise. 'I've got the rest of my unpacking to do. And, anyway, I haven't got a ticket.'

'Oh, yes, you have,' Hannah contradicted smugly. 'As soon as I knew you were coming to St Augustine's I bought you one. You can pay me back later!'

'Hannah!' Laura sighed. 'I won't be able to afford to pay you back until my wages come in and I can't afford the time to go.'

'Oh, phooey!' Hannah said rudely and screwed up her nose. 'It'll be a whole year until the next shindig, apart from a few boozy parties at Christmas. Can't you look on it as a way of celebrating the fact that we're working together again?'

Laura pulled an answering face. She'd never been much of a one for parties and formal Balls, and the last couple of years had been worse than ever. There honestly didn't seem to be much point in going through all the rituals of dating when there was no chance of anything coming of it.

'Please?' Hannah coaxed. 'You can keep me company.'

'What do you mean, keep you company? You hardly need me to hold your hand—you'll be swept off your feet all evening. Who's your escort for the evening? Leo Stirling?'

'Leo? Hardly!' Hannah hooted. 'If the word hadn't been hijacked by a certain section of the community, he'd be a prime example of your typical bachelor gay. A different woman every night, and every one a stunner.'

'Well, you're no wallflower! Is the man blind?'

'Far from it!' Hannah laughed. 'Thank you for the vote of confidence, but I've got my feet firmly planted on the ground. I've got far too much sense to think of taking him on—I'd only get trampled in the crush! Anyway, he's decided to go stag as he'll be fully occupied with running the auction part of the evening.'

'Even so,' Laura continued, 'I haven't been here long enough to find a suitable escort of my own. Perhaps, by next year. . .'

'If that's your excuse you've just lost the argument,' Hannah said smugly. 'At St Augustine's it's always been perfectly acceptable for groups of people to go to the Autumn Ball without being paired off in the traditional way. Some sensible person, years ago, decided it was more important for people to enjoy themselves while they help to raise money for good causes than to limit the numbers by imposing restrictions.'

Laura sighed, cursing silently as she realised that Hannah was slowly but surely demolishing every objection she voiced.

What made the whole situation worse was that the Laura whom Hannah had known would have given in with a smile. She didn't really have the heart to tell Hannah bluntly that things had changed since those days—that nowadays she just couldn't see the point of going to such gatherings.

While Laura tried to marshall her thoughts she glanced down at the watch pinned to the front of her mid-blue uniform and realised with a sense of relief that her break was all but over.

'Well, it's time to go back to the bedlam,' she said as she slipped her shoes back on and slid forward on the seat.

'Wait.' Hannah grabbed her by the elbow to stop her from standing up. 'Please, Laura,' she said earnestly, 'I would like you to come to the Ball with me. I think you'd enjoy it.'

Laura felt the frown pleating her forehead as she found herself fighting her natural inclinations in favour of giving in to Hannah's pleading. They'd been friends for so long and it was wonderful that they were back working together again. . .

'At least promise me that you'll think about it,' Hannah begged. 'It's just—you don't seem to be the same as you were when we last worked together. It's as if. . .as if it's an effort for you to laugh. . .as if you *need* to be taken out of yourself.'

'Neither of us are the same people we were when we first met,' Laura agreed, unsurprised by how observant her friend was but inwardly saddened by how accurate her words were.

As far as the rest of the world was concerned, she seemed to have learned how to cover up her feelings but Hannah had known her long enough to learn how to see below the surface, and evidently she hadn't lost the knack.

'You always were too sharp for your own good,' she grumbled good-naturedly. 'But you're right about the laughing. Sometimes it *is* hard to find things funny any more.'

'Well, you know you can always talk to me if you want to,' Hannah offered, all teasing put aside. 'I might have changed in some ways, but my ears still work just as well. Anyway, that's all the more reason to join me tonight,' she declared, her voice taking on an encouraging tone. 'Apart from anything else, it'll give you a chance to meet some of the other people you'll be working with in a more social atmosphere.'

'Enough! Enough!' Laura laughed as she finally made her escape. 'All I'm promising for now is that I'll think about it. . .OK?'

'OK,' Hannah conceded. 'But don't imagine that I won't be increasing the pressure the closer we get to the end of our shift. . .!'

It hadn't been an idle threat, either, Laura thought as she turned the hairdryer onto her freshly washed hair. All afternoon Hannah had been enlisting her friends to add their voices to the chorus of invitations.

Leo had been the funniest.

'Laura,' he'd said with an unaccustomed seriousness to his expression, 'I realise that you're a friend of Hannah's, and I freely admit that the thought of what she would do to me if I misbehaved is enough to strike terror into my manly heart, but. . .' he drew in an ostentatious breath '. . .if you come to the Ball, I hereby promise faithfully *not* to dance with you!'

She chuckled at the memory of the waggling eyebrows which had accompanied the declaration, then pulled a face at herself in the mirror.

Once again she was forced into the realisation that, in spite of her efforts at sophistication and her careful application of cosmetics, with her diminutive height and colouring and the short feathery style of her haircut she still looked rather like a slightly flustered elf.

She tugged at the top of her dress, but the boned bodice fitted her slender waist too well to allow her to pull it up any higher over the soft swell of her breasts. The forest-green shantung almost exactly matched her eyes, but the dark colour had the unfortunate effect of making her skin look almost as pale as milk—especially as there was so much of it on show. If only she had some of Hannah's natural colour.

'Are you ready yet?' Hannah's voice demanded from the other side of the door, and Laura reached for her small evening bag with a sigh.

'As ready as I'll ever be,' she admitted when she opened the door.

'Wow! I love the dress,' Hannah said, gesturing with one hand for Laura to turn around for her. 'Is it new?'

'Several years old, but this is the first time I've worn it. Yours is very sophisticated. The halter neck is so flattering and I love that shade of blue on you.' She deliberately turned Hannah's attention away, shutting her mind to the memory of the excitement she'd felt when she'd bought her own dress—the anticipation of the momentous occasion which had never happened. . .

Afraid that her thoughts would show on her face, she turned and reached for the lacy black shawl she'd put ready on the back of the chair.

'Well, our coach is ready and waiting,' Hannah began, then giggled when she realised what she'd said. 'Sounds like something out of a fairy story, doesn't it? Unfortunately this one's powered by diesel, not six white horses, and there's no guarantee that Prince Charming is going to appear tonight!'

'Actually, Hannah, I've decided to go in my car.'

'Laura!' her friend wailed. 'That means you're already planning on ducking out part way through the evening!'

'I'll have to, or I'll probably fall flat on my face,' Laura pointed out. 'I've still got half my unpacking to do and I've hardly had time to catch my breath at work before you've browbeaten me into going out for the evening.'

'Oh, well,' Hannah said with a resigned shrug as she stepped back out into the corridor and waited for her to lock the door. 'At least you're going to the Ball with me so I suppose I should be grateful.'

'Grateful enough to share the car with me to show me where this extravaganza is taking place?' Laura suggested.

'OK. We can let the rest know not to wait for us on our way out.' Hannah's good humour seemed to have reasserted itself as they made their way down the stairs of the nurses' accommodation, and she kept up a stream of cheerful chatter right through the journey.

Laura was glad she didn't have to do much more than supply the odd word. Between her concentration on navigating her way through the still-unfamiliar streets and her nerves at the prospect of walking into a room full of strangers, she couldn't spare any brain cells for following a conversation.

'It's a shame you had to park quite so far away from the entrance, but at least we found you a space under a light,' Hannah commented as they made their way into the spacious foyer of the country-house-styled hotel on the outskirts of town.

In seconds they were surrounded by the bright lights and cheerful hubbub of the gathering throng.

'Hannah?' Laura called, attracting her friend's attention as she made her way back from the cloakroom over two hours later. The meal was over, and she had no real interest in the auction part of the evening.

'Hi, Laura,' Hannah panted, still winded from her latest foray onto the dance floor. 'You can't be cold.' She gestured towards the shawl Laura had draped over one arm.

'No. It's warmed up a lot since everyone started dancing. Actually, I was thinking about leaving in a minute. I've already stayed much longer than I. . .'

'Laura. . .!' Hannah wailed. 'I thought you were enjoying yourself?'

'I was,' Laura hastened to reassure her. 'I have enjoyed myself—far more than I expected to—but. . .'

'You can't leave yet,' Hannah begged, her manner almost agitated.

As Laura watched Hannah glanced uneasily towards the easily recognisable gleam of Leo's head as he approached the rostrum. Although she had no idea why, Laura had the feeling that her friend was worried about something.

'The auction is about to start and there's still the draw to come. Can't you at least wait until then?' Hannah coaxed.

'Hannah. . .'

'Please? Pretty please?' Hannah said with her hands together as if she was pleading. 'In fact, if you stay until after the draw I'll be quite happy to travel back with you.'

'Don't be silly. You don't have to cut your own evening short just because I want to leave early.' Laura began to feel guilty. Was she really such a wet blanket?

'But you will stay until after the draw?'

Laura gave in gracefully, just as the loudspeaker burst to life.

'And now. . .' Leo began, and within seconds he had the room rocking with laughter as he teased and cajoled them out of their money as item after item came up for auction.

'He's so good at this,' Laura said as she wiped tears of mirth from her cheeks after Tina Wadland had successfully bid for the coveted free massage with the masseur of her choice.

'At least Leo now knows what he can do to earn a living if he decides he doesn't like being a doctor,' Hannah quipped, her own eyes bright with laughter.

Laura was fascinated by the byplay as Nicholas Prince began bidding hotly for the pledge of a week's holiday in a cottage in Brittany, and when Leo finally knocked it down to the A and E consultant she was even more fascinated to see the reaction of Sister Polly Lang, standing at his side.

'Hannah?' she said, careful to pitch her voice just for her friend's ears. 'Is there something going on between Dr Prince and Polly Lang?'

'Not much,' Hannah said cryptically, and glanced around cagily before she leant closer. 'Just that they're getting married tomorrow. The cottage is probably where he's taking her for their honeymoon.'

'Really?' Laura exclaimed and turned to look over her shoulder again at the couple, standing near the back of the room. She'd hardly had time to get to know them as new colleagues, but a warm feeling of pleasure filled her when she saw the way they were looking at each other—pleasure mixed with just a little touch of envy, perhaps.

'No one said anything about it today,' she commented with a frown. 'You'd think I'd have heard something on the grapevine. . .'

'Shh!' Hannah nudged her in warning. 'I'll tell you more later—it's all a bit secret.' Her eyes were bright with suppressed glee. 'Aren't you glad you stayed now?'

'All right. All right. I've thoroughly enjoyed myself so

I give you permission to say it,' Laura said with a smile, resignation in her voice.

'What? You don't mean, "I told you so", do you? As if I would!'

They were both laughing when a drumroll silenced the hubbub of conversation which had followed the last of the auctioned pledges.

'Oh, good. It's time for the draw.' Laura watched as Hannah anticipated the next announcement and rummaged in her evening bag to withdraw the tickets, comparing the serial numbers on both of them before handing one to her.

'Here. This one's yours,' she announced, with another strange glance towards Leo.

Laura just had time to register that her friend seemed almost furtive when Leo began his patter.

'Now we come to the last of tonight's star prizes so will all you lovely ladies take out your tickets and keep an eye on the numbers because *this* is what you could be winning!'

As Laura craned to see between the heads and shoulders of the people who had suddenly clustered in front of her, she cursed the fact that, even in her highest heels, she still felt as if she must be one of the shortest people in the room.

The women around her had erupted into a chorus of shouts and wolf-whistles of approval, but she still couldn't see what they were looking at.

'Hey! Hannah!' She tugged her friend's elbow, having to shout to be heard over all the noise. 'What's going on?'

Hannah glanced back at her and suddenly seemed to realise her problem, stepping to one side to allow Laura her first clear view of the front of the room.

The lights had been dimmed, a single spotlight now

illuminating the stage area where a solitary man stood in silence.

At first glance he seemed to be dressed in an impeccable evening suit like the rest of the men in the room but, unlike them, his hair was just a little too long, the dark silky tendrils almost brushing his broad shoulders.

The final touch was a jet-black domino mask which partially obscured his face and lent him an almost sinister air of danger.

As Laura gazed at him, almost mesmerised by his strange stillness in the face of the bedlam in the room, her heartbeat gave the first skip of awareness in several long years. She tried to drag her eyes away but she couldn't stop them running over him as he stood there with the arrogance of a superb wild animal.

In the stark black of his traditional evening suit he was the epitome of tall, dark and handsome as he stood there with his fists braced on his lean hips with an almost insolent swagger.

'Ladies! Ladies!' Leo called, and Laura saw the white gleam of his teeth as he smiled. 'You'll make the rest of us men jealous if you continue like that!'

The chorus turned to cat-calls until he held up a dark fabric bag and, with all the aplomb of a fairground showman, delved one hand inside and pulled out a square of white paper with a flourish.

'And the winner is. . .number two hundred and nineteen,' he declared.

The announcement was greeted with a chorus of moans and groans as each of the women eagerly checked their tickets. When there was no triumphant cry everyone started looking around at their neighbour.

'Don't be shy, now,' Leo said in a coaxing tone. 'He'll only bite if you ask him to.'

'Well, he won't be nibbling on me—my number is miles out,' Hannah declared as she turned towards Laura, her eyes almost feverishly bright. 'What number were you?'

Laura had been too busy watching the events around her to bother checking her own ticket. She'd never won at any game of chance and had given up trying long ago, but just out of interest she turned her ticket over and tilted it towards the brightly lit stage to decipher the numbers stamped in the corner.

'It's you!' Hannah squealed when she saw the number over her shoulder. 'It's your ticket!'

Her voice was loud enough to travel right through the murmuring throng and before Laura could follow her inclination to thrust the offending evidence into her friend's hand a path had magically opened up in front of her and hands were reaching out to touch her, guiding her reluctant feet towards the front of the room.

'Hello!' Leo greeted her, his voice as hearty as ever, although he seemed slightly puzzled by her presence, his eyes glancing over the top of her head and into the crowd behind her.

'Who is this lucky lady?' he demanded jovially as he reached for the ticket she was still clutching tightly in her hand, and she emerged from her horrified trance just long enough to hand it to him.

'Lucky?' she echoed faintly, hating the feeling that she was the focus of so many eyes, then realised that she hadn't given him an answer. 'I. . .I'm Laura,' she stammered.

'Well, Lucky Laura, are you ready to claim your prize?' Leo stepped aside and Laura's senses were assailed by her first close-up view of the man standing in the spotlight.

For just a few seconds she had actually thought of asking Leo to draw again, but the words 'No, thank you,' remained for ever frozen in her throat as she met the stranger's eyes for the first time.

They were a pale icy blue and were fixed unerringly on her own, sending a shiver of atavistic awareness up the back of her neck.

Somewhere music started playing and she saw him blink, as though the sound had taken him by surprise, before he straightened up, his chin going up a notch as he held out one lean hand towards her.

For several long seconds she found herself looking from his hand to his eyes and back again while the music played on.

She hadn't bothered to find out any of the details of this part of the evening—hadn't expected to stay long enough to find out.

What was supposed to happen now?

What did he want her to do?

Leo's helping hand under her elbow drew her into the bright circle of light before he disappeared into the surrounding darkness.

From the moment she'd met the masked man's eyes for the first time he hadn't allowed her to look away, the intensity of his icy blue gaze holding her prisoner so that she felt as if they were somehow connected within the encircling prison of the spotlight.

The music changed and slowly he started to move with the new rhythm. Not dancing, exactly. More a matter of shifting his weight, swaying and twisting his torso as if he was testing his muscles. One shoulder rotated forward and shrugged, followed by the other and then the stark black of his jacket was sliding backwards and down.

She'd assumed that he was dressed in the same impeccable way as the other men but as soon as the jacket fell away from the width of his shoulders she realised that, apart from the black bow at his throat, the only clothing remaining on the upper half of his body was a waistcoat shot through with gleaming metallic threads.

The roar of approval which greeted this manoeuvre broke the spell he'd woven around her.

Suddenly Laura remembered that they *weren't* alone and she felt the heat of embarrassment surge up into her face.

'Laura. . .?'

She saw his mouth form the word as he held out his hand towards her again. This time he took the single step which brought her within reach, and she found herself placing her hand in his.

He tightened his fingers around hers and pulled gently, and she gave in to the pressure as he drew her into his arms.

'Relax,' he whispered, his mouth close to her ear as he captured her other hand and lifted both of them up to his shoulders.

'How?' she whispered back as her hands clenched nervously on the glimmering fabric. She thought she heard him suppress a snort of laughter but, with the sound of the music and the cat-calls and wolf-whistles of the audience surrounding them, she couldn't be sure.

'Link your hands behind my neck and follow my lead,' he whispered and, grateful for the suggestion, she did, sliding her fingers tentatively under the silky strands of his long dark hair to clasp them together.

As soon as he released her hands he stroked the backs

of his fingers down her arms, his hands cupping her shoulders as he drew her against his body so that she couldn't help following the same hypnotic rhythm.

She'd once seen a couple dancing the lambada and she remembered thinking that it was one of the most blatantly sexual dances she'd ever watched—but this was something else. . .

As he'd drawn her against his body he'd widened his stance so that they were now moving together with one of his thighs pressed firmly into the cradle of her body and one of hers trapped firmly between his.

She felt almost surrounded by him—his size, his strength, his heat—and she looked up into his face, helpless to resist his powerful physical magnetism.

Even though he was wearing the mysterious mask she could see enough of his face to know that he was a handsome man, his eyes very pale for such tanned skin and his eyelashes sinfully long and dark.

'You're good,' he murmured in her ear, and his arms tightened around her until there wasn't a breath of space between their bodies.

Laura was stunned to realise how easily she'd been following his lead, moving to the insistent beat of the music as if they'd rehearsed it all before, even though it had been several years since she'd danced at all—and she'd *never* danced like this before.

Without realising that she'd done it, her head had come to rest in the curve of his shoulder, and a deep shudder of awareness had her tightening her own hold on him when he nuzzled the soft flesh of her exposed throat.

'Hold tight,' he warned as the music finally drew to a close, and she just had time to draw in a sharp gasp of

breath as one of his hands slid down intimately to the curve
of her bottom and the other angled across her back to clasp
her shoulder.

Before she realised what he was going to do he'd tilted
her backwards over his arm into a classic pose, and his
mouth had swooped down to cover hers in a brief but
utterly electric kiss.

CHAPTER TWO

'WAIT!'

In spite of the command, Laura's pace hardly faltered as she hurried across the car park towards her car, shivering as the chill of the November night struck her over-heated flesh.

She'd never heard his voice properly—just whispers and murmurs in her ear, almost drowned out by the surrounding din. Even so, she knew the identity of the husky voice, calling out to her through the darkness, and she didn't want to have anything further to do with him. . .didn't dare.

As she slid the key into the lock she blessed the fact that she'd had them ready in her hand. After what had just happened between them on the stage she'd been half expecting this to happen, especially as she'd had to tear herself out of his arms, but she'd thought that at least she'd have a little more time than this to make her escape.

Her stomach clenched when she thought of her undignified flight across the crowded room. Her face still felt as if it must be lit up like a neon sign, but she forced herself to block the thought out of her mind.

If she didn't concentrate on getting her crabby old Mini started he would catch up with her before she could get away.

Once she got back to her room there would be plenty of time to replay the shocking events of the evening. . .

when she wasn't worried about coming face to face with *him* again.

'Thank you, thank you,' she said fervently, sighing with relief when the engine coughed into action. Even so, she couldn't help casting one last look over her shoulder before she turned out onto the road—just as the tall figure reached the empty space where her car had stood.

This time it was a streetlight which illuminated the taut muscles in his naked shoulders and arms, highlighting the ghostly halo that the cold night air made of his rapid breathing and drawing metallic gleams from the exotic fabric of his waistcoat as he threw his jacket down in disgust.

That must be why he'd been able to reach the car park so quickly—he'd done little more than grab his discarded jacket from the stage before he'd followed her. He was even still wearing that stupid mask, for heaven's sake.

The silence inside the tiny car was broken by the semi-hysterical giggle which escaped from her as she accelerated away. Who did he think he was? The Lone Ranger?

Laura groaned when her alarm went off the next morning. She felt as if she hadn't slept at all, what with the endless mental replays of the events of last night and her guilty denial of her reaction to it. . .to *him*.

What a way to get to know her new colleagues—to be dragged up on a stage to dance with a half-naked man and then make an utter fool of herself when he kissed her for a finale.

Everything would have been all right if only she hadn't responded so fervently and then, when she'd realised that he'd become every bit as aroused as she had, she'd lost her nerve and run like a scared rabbit.

Her face flamed again as she remembered the chorus of whistles and applause which had filled the room when he'd held her all-too-willing body against the stark masculine power of his.

When the noise surrounding them had brought her to her senses all she'd been interested in was grabbing her shawl and bag from Hannah and getting out of there.

Now all she had to do was turn up for her shift in the accident and emergency department and pretend that the whole thing had never happened. . .and keep her fingers crossed that something else cropped up quickly to keep the hospital grapevine busy.

Perhaps the new doctor due to start in A and E today to cover for Nicholas Prince's absence would occupy everyone's wagging tongues—and keep her own mind off the fact that the hormones which she'd thought had ceased to function seemed to have been kick-started into a full-throttled roar.

At least she wouldn't have to face Hannah's inquisition until later. She and Leo had both managed to arrange to have the morning off in order to act as witnesses at Polly's marriage to Nick Prince. Neither of them would be on duty until the afternoon.

The brisk walk through the crisp chill of the morning from her room in the nurses' accommodation to the A and E department was just long enough for her to get herself under control. She was guiltily glad that her arrival coincided with the banshee wail of two ambulances so that she was pitchforked straight into activity.

Her own charge was a little girl of six, the paramedic all but running beside her as she was wheeled into the emergency room.

He had one hand pressing firmly on the child's femoral artery, high up on the skinny little leg, compressing it against her pelvis in an attempt to control the massive blood loss.

'Severe trauma to right leg about four inches below the knee—pretty close to complete amputation,' reported Ted Larrabee as he handed over. 'She's bleeding profusely and very shocked so we had to put a tourniquet on as well, and we've managed to get three IVs into her and they're running wide open.'

'Oh, God. . .' Laura breathed as she swiftly completed the task of connecting up the dainty child to the hospital monitoring systems and got her first look at the extent of the injuries.

Whatever had happened, it had chopped through skin, muscle and bone until the lower part of her leg looked as if it was hanging on by little more than a narrow band of flesh.

There was a warning call and all those without the heavy protective aprons stood back while the first X-ray was taken, then stepped forward again in an elaborately choreographed dance to continue their own tasks while the next plate was positioned.

'How the hell did *this* happen?' a deep husky voice demanded, and all the hairs went up on the back of Laura's neck.

There wasn't time to do more than flick a swift glance over the man beside her and determine the fact that she hadn't met him before, then she blocked her strange reaction to him out of her mind and concentrated on the task in hand.

'She was being dropped off at school and started to get

out of the wrong side of the car,' Ted detailed succinctly. 'An oncoming car couldn't help ploughing into the open door and shut it on her leg.'

Laura wasn't the only one to gasp as the graphic image flashed across her mind, but there wasn't time to dwell on it.

There were blood samples to be cross-matched and supplies to be confirmed for the duration of the child's extensive trip to Theatre. Time was of the essence now, with every wasted minute compromising the healthy survival of the leg tissues deprived of blood and lessening the chances that the limb could be reattached successfully.

Out of the corner of her eye she saw a second dark-haired man arrive on the scene, and the two of them conferred briefly in front of the X-ray view-box.

'Good,' muttered Celia MacDonald beside her. 'If the poor wee thing's got Alex Marshall working on her she stands a better than average chance—he's a damn good orthopod.'

Laura blinked. She knew from what Hannah had already told her about their superior that Big Mac rarely said two words where one would do so this was praise indeed.

It wasn't long before the youngster had been stabilised enough to be taken out of their hands and on her way to Theatre, where the team was waiting to begin the long task of piecing her together again.

As Laura had guessed, Alex had confirmed that although it would be a three-dimensional jigsaw to put together the time-consuming plating and screwing together of her shattered leg would be the simplest part of the task.

He'd been the first to admit that it was the hours of microsurgery the six-year-old would require to rejoin her

crushed and mangled nerves and veins which would determine whether her leg could be saved—and how much use
it would be to her.

Laura had finished her clearing-up duties and had just
turned to leave the room when she cannoned straight into
a large, dark-haired immovable obstruction and began to
lose her balance.

'I—I'm sorry!' she stammered as she tried to find her
feet, but when she went to take a step back her elbows
were firmly held in the hands which had saved her from
disaster.

Startled, she looked up over a smoothly shaven chin and
slightly lopsided grin into a pair of strangely familiar pale
blue eyes. When she saw that they were surrounded by
sinfully long black lashes her breath caught in her throat.

Her eyes flew over the neatly barbered dark hair, then
took in the pristine shirt and tie, framed by his conservative
dark suit, and for a second she almost doubted the evidence
of her own eyes.

Then she gazed up again and a newly familiar shiver of
awareness skated right up the length of her spine to raise
all the hairs on the back of her neck as she realised that
she *did* recognise those unforgettable eyes.

'The Lone Ranger, I presume,' she murmured, and was
surprised to see him flinch.

Suddenly she realised what she'd done, and she could
have bitten her tongue off. She closed her eyes briefly as
a flush of embarrassment filled her face, and she knew that
those few words had ruined her chance of ever denying
that she'd recognised him.

Her gaze meshed with his, and she was helpless to drag
her eyes away until she caught sight of an answering heat

washing over the leanly sculpted cheek-bones she hadn't
seen under the domino mask last night.

'For God's sake, keep your voice down,' he muttered, his
dark eyebrows drawing down into a deep V. He suddenly
seemed to realise that he was still holding her elbows and
released them hastily to swing a haunted glance around the
room. 'I hope you haven't told anybody? Leo promised
you could be trusted.'

'How could I tell anyone?' she murmured, grateful that
he'd finally broken the physical connection between them.
She was stung by the accusation in his tone and more than
a little puzzled by his reference to Leo. 'I've only just
recognised you...and what's Leo got to do with it?'

'He's the one who picked you...supposedly because
you were trustworthy,' he repeated, visibly agitated. 'He
must have told you how important it was to keep it quiet?'

'No. Why would he tell me that?'

'Because of my position here, of course,' he snapped as
if the answer should have been obvious.

'Well, if you were that worried about people's reaction
to your little sideline perhaps you shouldn't have offered
to do it,' she snapped back, hard pushed to keep her
voice down.

'I didn't,' he snarled, and ran one agitated hand over his
newly shorn hair, visibly startled when he realised how
short it now was. 'It isn't a sideline. I was badgered into
it—by Leo!'

'But. . .'

'Look. . .'

Laura saw him draw in a steadying breath and when she
realised just how worked up he was she decided to hold
her tongue and give him first shot at explaining.

'Apparently, the chap he had lined up to do that dance thing had his appendix taken out yesterday—here in St Augustine's—and that meant Leo was stuck for someone to do his finale.'

'And he twisted your arm?' she ventured as she began to understand the sequence of events.

'With the promise that no one would be able to recognise me, and that he'd try to find some way of fixing it so that the person chosen was someone utterly trustworthy.'

'And, instead, you got me,' she said softly, and saw him grow visibly paler.

'You mean, you *aren't* the person he asked?' he said with more than a touch of panic in his voice. 'Then how did you know who I was?'

'I recognised your eyes,' she replied, grateful that he would never know about the strange awareness she seemed to have developed about his presence. When he'd joined her beside their little patient the hairs had gone up on the back of her neck before she'd even caught sight of his icy blue eyes. 'They're an unusual colour against your tanned skin and dark hair.'

'But I was wearing that stupid mask last night,' he pointed out agitatedly. 'Leo said that would stop anyone recognising me afterwards.'

Words seemed to fail him as she shook her head, and for a moment she thought about drawing out the agony but relented.

'Don't forget, apart from Leo, I was the only one to get close to you,' she reminded him gently. 'And you won't have to worry about me talking because I've got just as much reason to want the whole thing kept quiet as you have.'

He gazed down at her for a moment before he answered, as if he was gauging her sincerity, 'So, perhaps we should make a pact to watch each other's backs?' he suggested with the hint of a smile.

'Sounds good enough for me,' Laura said with an answering smile, and offered her hand. 'Laura Kirkland. Newly appointed Staff Nurse, A and E, St Augustine's Hospital. Second day here.'

'Well, you're one day up on me, Laura Kirkland,' he said as he enveloped her small hand in the warmth of his and held it just a little longer than necessary. 'Wolff Bergen, at your service.'

'Wolff?' She couldn't help the way the thread of laughter gave a lilt to her voice.

'Yes, Wolff. And I've already heard all the jokes,' he said wearily as he turned towards the door. 'Unfortunately, it's a family name on my father's side and I got landed with it.'

'I like it,' Laura decided as she walked out through the door he held open for her, her head tilted on one side as she looked up at him. 'I think it suits you, especially since you've had your hair cut—or was that a wig last night?'

'Hush,' he cautioned softly with a quick glance both ways down the corridor. 'I think *that* had better be a topic of conversation we agree to limit to discussion outside the hospital.'

In other words, topic closed, Laura said to herself as she followed him along the corridor, his long legs carrying him further and further ahead.

Ah, well, it was probably for the best. She wasn't in a position to start any relationships and even if the reciprocal attraction she'd seen in his eyes persuaded him to begin pursuing her he was far too good-looking to hang around waiting for long once she showed him she wasn't interested.

She tamped down the unhappy ache into the shadowy corner inside her heart which it had occupied for so long now, and straightened her shoulders with new determination. This was the second day of her new post at St Augustine's, and if Hannah's recommendations were anything to go on she could look forward to a long and happy career here.

She would just have to be satisfied with what she could have, rather than what she wanted.

The trouble was that she couldn't switch her mind off, and by the time Hannah came in to work she had a whole list of pointed questions to ask her about the events of the previous evening.

Unfortunately, before she had time to corner her friend Hannah was surrounded by half the staff in the department.

'Is it true?' Tina demanded eagerly. 'Is Polly getting married to Old Nick?'

For a second Hannah looked almost taken aback, as if this was the last question she had expected, but then she smiled broadly when she realised that somehow the secret was out.

'Yes!' she confirmed with glee. 'Polly married her Prince at eleven-thirty this morning.'

'And they asked you to be a witness?' demanded another voice.

'Leo and me, and then we joined them for a celebratory meal afterwards,' she elaborated.

'Oh, I think it's so romantic, especially the way they managed to keep it all a secret.'

'From *some* of us,' Hannah pointed out with a grin.

She was being so unbearably smug about the fact that she'd been in on the secret that Laura longed to take her down a peg or two with a few sharp words of her own about trustworthiness, but she'd have to wait until she could get her alone.

There was no way she was going to have her own private concerns turned into grist for the rumour mill.

But later, when there were no other ears around. . .

She turned away from the chattering group and went back to the reception area. If nothing else, she could always find work to occupy her hands, even if it was the nauseating job of soaking off a pair of toxic socks which had all but welded themselves to the feet of the elderly lady she took through to the cubicle.

'Oh, Maggie, what have you done to yourself?' she chided the elderly bag lady gently. First, she'd soaked the malodorous feet in a povidone-iodine solution and now she was patiently picking the remaining rotting threads of a pair of disintegrated socks out of her heavily infected flesh.

'Me boots got wet, missy, and I didn't have any dry ones to put on.'

Laura glanced wryly at the sodden wrecks, lying abandoned under the edge of the trolley. She'd actually had to cut one of them apart to get it off so Maggie wouldn't be wearing *them* any more. When she'd finished this part of the job and applied antibiotic dressings she'd have to make some quick enquiries about St Augustine's connections with local charity shops—or perhaps they had a cupboard somewhere with oddments of clothing donated or left behind.

'Where have you been staying, Maggie?' she asked

gently when she noticed that her A and E form was incomplete. 'Is there someone we can contact to tell them you'll be staying in hospital for a few days?'

'No point cos I'm not staying,' the elderly woman replied aggressively. 'Anyway, why d'you want to know where I live, missy? Going to come and visit me, then?'

'I was just hoping it wasn't too far away for you to come back to have your feet dressed,' Laura said calmly. 'You're going to need to have them attended to regularly for a while or they might turn really nasty.'

'It's not that far away,' she said stoically. 'I'll get here one way or 'nother. Got to be able to walk, see. Else I can't get me soup from the kitchen by the station.'

'Right. Well, if you'd like to keep your feet up there for a minute I'll just see if there's a spare cup of tea going begging. Do you want sugar in yours?'

''Ow much?' she challenged with a scowl, one hand covering the bulging carrier bag she'd held clutched to her side throughout.

'This one'll be free, Maggie, my love, but you'll have to smile at me if you want another one,' Laura quipped.

'Depends what it tastes like whether I'll *want* another one, missy. . .and I take three sugars.'

'Three it is.' Laura nodded and drew the curtain across behind her as she marvelled at the old lady's amazing resilience. Her feet must have been causing her agony for ages before she'd finally given in and asked for help.

She went back with the tea quite quickly, but it took a little longer to sort out the problem of new footwear.

In the end, she turned to Sister MacDonald and explained the circumstances, telling her that she hadn't tried too hard to persuade Maggie to allow herself to be admitted.

'You're quite right,' the senior sister agreed. 'We know Maggie of old and there's little chance that you'll get her to agree to stay in here, even though she'd be in comfort while her feet heal. She's too independent. As for the problem of replacement footwear. . .' She reached for the telephone, paused in thought for a second and started dialling.

'Now, then, Maggie,' Laura said when she finally returned to the cubicle with the new footwear tucked out of sight under one arm. 'I've got a bit of a problem and I need you to help me out.'

'Me, missy?' she questioned warily, one hand still wrapped tightly round the empty mug while the other clutched her precious bag of belongings on her lap. 'What d'you want?'

'Well, I had such trouble getting your boots off that I ruined one of them.' She picked up the offending article and showed it to the old lady, holding her breath so that she didn't have to breathe in the awful smell emanating from it.

'You made a proper old mess of that and no mistake,' Maggie grumbled.

'I'm sorry,' Laura said as she deposited it again as far away as possible. 'I'm hoping you'll accept these in exchange—so that I won't get into trouble for spoiling yours.'

She saw the flash of acquisitiveness in the old lady's faded blue eyes when she caught sight of the footwear Laura was offering. They weren't new but they'd been well looked after and were sound and watertight, and Big Mac had even scrounged up a couple of pairs of socks to go with them.

'Well, I s'pose I can take 'em if it stops you from getting

a flea in your ear—mind, you'd better not ruin these ones when I come back to get the dressings changed,' she warned as she gingerly pulled the socks over the fresh white dressings, then posted her feet into the new boots and laced them up.

'If you'll promise to come back for every appointment I'll promise not to spoil your boots,' Laura bargained.

'I bet you'll forget 'ow many sugars I take in me tea,' she challenged with a wicked grin.

'Three, stirred clockwise, you terrible woman. Now let me get you out of here so I can have a bit of peace.'

She offered a helping hand as Maggie slid over the edge of the bed and found her feet, then drew the curtain back while she gathered up her meagre belongings.

'Missy?' The old lady had paused to look back. 'Thanks. You've got a good heart. . .lousy tea, mind, but a good heart.'

Laura was still laughing when she came out of the cubicle with a tightly tied plastic bag.

'Maggie's boots?' Wolff grinned as he nodded towards the burden she was holding at arm's length, his eyes gleaming down at her.

'How did you guess?' Laura asked with a grimace. 'I thought I'd captured all the smell inside the bag.'

'I heard the whole saga from next door.' He tilted his dark head towards the next cubicle. 'It helped to take my client's mind off the fact that I was having to stitch the back of his hand together after his girlfriend's cat's claws had ripped it open.'

'Glad to have provided some entertainment, but now it's time for my break—and I won't be having tea!'

'I'm due to put my feet up, too,' he said as he began

walking beside her. 'Speaking of entertainment,' he continued, lowering his voice, 'has anyone said anything to you?'

Laura knew immediately that he was talking about last night's events and she felt the beginnings of a blush work its way up her throat.

'Nothing so far. Everyone seems far more interested in talking about Nick's and Polly's marriage. Anyway, Hannah's been kept busy since she started her shift.'

'Interesting, the way you said her name through gritted teeth,' he said musingly, one dark eyebrow arching up towards his hair as he folded his arms across his chest and leant back against the work surface in the kitchenette. 'I take it that she's the one who *should* have joined me up on the stage last night.'

'Yes. And I'm almost certain that the switch was deliberate,' she added heatedly as she checked the water level in the kettle and switched it on. 'Just wait till I give her a piece of my mind.'

'Was my dancing that bad?' he challenged softly, his voice just that bit deeper and huskier as he leant towards her in the confined space. 'I got the distinct impression that you had really entered into the spirit of the thing— especially by the time we got to the finale. . .'

'Don't. . .' Laura covered her face with her hands, mortified that he had realised how much she had been affected by him.

'Hey! I was there too, remember? It was pretty explosive stuff!'

'But I don't *do* that sort of thing!' Laura exclaimed, rounding on him.

'What sort of thing? Dance? Enjoy yourself—?'

'Make an exhibition of myself,' she butted in, hoping to stop him speaking, but his eyes were gleaming with unholy glee as he completed his list of suggestions with one which robbed her of breath.

'Respond sexually to a complete stranger?'

'Oh, God,' she breathed, her eyes wide with horror as she gazed up into an icy blue that seared her like a laser with the knowledge they contained.

She'd hoped that he hadn't realised exactly how much her body had responded to his—after all, a woman's arousal wasn't as blatantly obvious as a man's...as *his* had been. But no such luck.

'If you were a gentleman you wouldn't have said that,' she enunciated through stiff lips as she dragged her eyes away and closed them in mortification. She could almost feel the colour draining out of her face.

'Ah,' he said silkily, 'whatever gave you the idea that I was a gentleman? In fact, I don't think I *want* to be a gentleman if it means I have to pretend that I didn't enjoy the sensation of having you in my arms and. . .'

'Don't. . . Please!' she begged. 'I don't. . .I'm not. . .'

An arrested expression crossed his face.

'You're not married, are you?' he demanded. 'Or engaged?'

'No,' she wailed. 'It's nothing like that.'

'Then where's the problem?' he said, suddenly far too cheerful for her liking. 'I'm single, you're single and we're both normal, healthy human beings.'

'Speak for yourself,' she retorted bitterly, then whirled away from him as several years of suppressed emotions threatened to overflow. 'I'm sorry. I've got to go,' she muttered and hurried out of the room just as the kettle began to scream.

'Laura?' he called after her as the door swung shut behind her, and she nearly laughed. That was the second time she'd ended up running away from him, for all the good it would do her.

'Hey, Laura! Got time for a coffee?' Hannah asked with a breezy smile when they all but collided in the corridor.

'Not just at the moment,' Laura replied tightly, hardly glancing towards her startled friend as she continued rapidly on her way.

One part of her wanted to let fly at Hannah for dumping her into such an embarrassing situation without any warning, but she was so upset at the moment that she didn't trust herself not to explode.

It had been bad enough last night when she had thought it was just her bad luck to have her number pulled out of the bag, but now that she knew that Hannah had done it on purpose she felt as if she'd been betrayed.

There hadn't been time since she'd moved to St Augustine's to talk to Hannah about all the reasons which had made her change her speciality from Paediatrics to A and E, or the circumstances which had made her decide to move to another hospital.

Even so, she had thought that Hannah had been a good enough friend not to risk hurting her like that.

She'd almost reached the entrance to the reception area when raised voices dragged her out of her thoughts. Through the glass-paned door she caught sight of the flash of light on what must surely be a seven- or eight-inch blade and she froze, all her own problems instantly forgotten.

CHAPTER THREE

'COME on, now, son. Put it down,' said a voice just out of Laura's sight in the L-shaped area. 'We don't want anyone getting hurt.'

'Speak for yourself, old man,' retorted a strident male voice. 'You can't tell me what to do.'

'It's my job to make certain people don't get hurt in here,' said the first voice, his words admirably calm and measured amid the furore, and Laura suddenly realised that he must be the member of the hospital security force who was on duty in the accident and emergency department.

'Well, it doesn't look as if you're doing much of a job today,' taunted the youngster, whose strutting progress around one end of the waiting area had just brought him back into Laura's view.

He could hardly have been more than twenty-two or -three—possibly much younger—and although Laura had never seen him before his uniform was becoming increasingly familiar, with his scruffy drab clothing and his matted hair hanging in stringy disarray across feverishly bright eyes in an unhealthily pale face.

The thing which drew most of her attention, though, was the wicked-looking knife he held in one hand, the gleaming blade the only well-cared-for item he seemed to possess.

Out of the corner of her eye Laura caught sight of a movement and turned her head slowly to see Sister MacDonald, signalling surreptitiously for her to get help.

43

Laura nodded once, careful not to draw attention to herself, and waited just long enough for the young man's next shambling journey to take him out of sight before she spun round and sprinted silently away.

She assumed that the security guard followed the same practice as the staff at her last hospital, and that he was carrying an alarm to call for assistance. Unfortunately, she realised that if he'd been taken unawares when this thug had pulled out his knife he might not have had time to activate it.

The same was true of any panic button situated by the admissions desk. She'd known other incidents where the staff had been so concerned for the safety of those closest to the threat of danger that they'd delayed just too long before they thought to activate it.

'*I'm* the one with the knife and I know how to use it, too,' shouted the increasingly agitated youngster, his chilling words echoing along the corridor towards Laura, just before she smacked the next set of fire doors open with both hands and barrelled into the staffroom.

'Hannah,' she gasped, relieved to see that her friend hadn't disappeared. 'How can I find out whether the silent panic button has been activated for the reception area? There's a nutter out there, threatening people with a knife!'

The welcoming smile on Hannah's face changed instantly to one of concern as she leapt to her feet and reached for the internal phone.

A second figure straightened up equally quickly from a comfortable sprawl, and Laura realised that Wolff must have stayed to drink his cup of coffee after all.

'Has anyone been hurt?' he demanded as he strode towards her.

'Not as far as I could see, but I wasn't actually in the room,' she explained as she led the way rapidly out of the room.

Hannah was now speaking to someone on the other end of the phone, and Laura blessed the fact that at least one of them had been at the hospital long enough to know the system.

Once again Wolff's longer stride enabled him to draw ahead of Laura, and she had to sprint to catch up with him and grab his arm before he got too close to the reinforced glass panels in the door.

'Wait a minute,' she breathed, suddenly stupidly aware of the strength in the leanly muscular forearm she was holding. 'Can you see what's going on in there now?'

Peering round his shoulder, she could see that everyone was still frozen in the same places as when she'd left. Celia MacDonald nodded briefly to let them know that she knew they were there and was ready to react when needed.

They listened for a moment and, to Laura's relief, little seemed to have changed since she'd fled for help, except the excitability of the young tough and the increasingly incoherent violence of his language.

As far as they could tell, he was still marching erratically about and still brandishing the lethal blade in people's faces, obviously relishing the way they cringed away as he brought the razor edge closer and closer.

'I've got to find some way of distracting him or he's going to take it too far,' Wolff muttered, his voice a husky rumble next to her ear and his dark brows drawn tightly into a frown of concentration.

'Well, you can't just walk in there,' Laura objected. 'In your white coat you're just another authority figure and you could tip him right over the edge.'

Wolff froze for a moment in deep thought, then threw her an unexpectedly wicked grin and sent her pulse rate into overdrive.

'Clever girl! That's the answer!' he whispered jubilantly as he began stripping off the tell-tale white coat.

'What on earth. . .?' Laura began, but he didn't even pause to explain as he continued to pull his burgundy patterned tie askew and undid several buttons on his pristine white shirt.

'Quick,' he directed. 'Help me to look dishevelled—as if I've been in a fight or something. . .'

Laura wasn't certain what was going on but she grabbed one side of his shirt and yanked it out of the waistband of his trousers before she undid the cuff of one sleeve and left it flapping.

'Like that?' she asked softly, overwhelmingly aware of the scent of soap and man which surrounded her. 'What a shame you got rid of that wild hair of yours. . .'

'Enough about the hair,' he said with a swift flash of white teeth, and she suddenly realised that he was almost enjoying himself.

'Now listen,' he continued as he kept one eye on the events on the other side of the door. 'When he comes up this end again where there are fewer people I'm going to burst through the doors as if I'm being chased. I want you to come flying in after me, shouting the odds, and with any luck the little toad will be distracted long enough for the security man to take him down.'

'OK.' Laura nodded and drew in a quick breath to calm her roiling stomach. 'But, please, be careful,' she whispered.

She didn't know where the words had come from but suddenly realised that she didn't want him to be injured.

'Why, Laura, I didn't know you cared!' he teased with a quick heart-stopping grin, then his eyes lost their glint as he faced the door again, waiting for their quarry to come into view.

Laura watched as he held one hand up with three fingers extended for Celia MacDonald to see. When she calmly nodded and surreptitiously copied his signal Laura realised that she was actually relaying the message on to the beleagured security man.

She drew in a deep breath to calm herself as Wolff removed first one digit then another in a silent countdown before he slammed both hands forcefully against the doors and hit the room at a run.

Afterwards, Laura couldn't remember what she'd shouted during the bedlam of the ensuing five seconds. All she knew was that it felt like a thousand years as she watched the courageous security guard seize the opportunity to run up behind the distracted thug and attempt to bind his arms harmlessly at his sides.

Even then his wiry opponent was struggling and screaming obscenities, and before Wolff could get close enough to lend assistance he made one final desperate lunge with his pinioned arms to try to force his captor to release him.

'Oh, my God!' shrieked the woman closest to the heart of the action. 'He's stabbed himself!'

For several seconds there was an almost deathly silence as everyone stared in awful fascination at the spreading tide of red which began to pour down the young man's legs.

'Trolley. . .quick!' Wolff snapped, his voice overriding the wailing curse of disbelief and pain that the young thug let out when he realised what he had done to himself.

'He's losing his viscera,' Laura warned when she saw the dark shiny protrusion of the young man's intestines through the slash in his disreputable clothing, and she dashed towards him.

'Get him horizontal—now!'

The command in Wolff's voice was totally at odds with his dishevelled appearance and brought instant results.

Within seconds the bully boy was surrounded by the very people he had been threatening, but instead of meting out retribution they were working as fast as they could to save his life.

As soon as he'd been whisked into the emergency room he was pounced on from all sides, his clothes efficiently stripped away and a wet dressing applied to cover and protect the protruding contents of his abdomen while several IV lines were inserted and some O-negative blood started.

A quick telephone call warned Theatre what to expect, and he was on his way.

'Well done, everyone,' Wolff said as he finally stripped off his blood-spattered disposables and dumped them. 'Now, I think I'd better go back out there and let them know that the crazies haven't completely taken over here.'

There was a round of laughter as the team realised that some of the poor people who had been terrorised by their erstwhile patient might not have realised what had been going on earlier when Wolff had burst in amongst them.

'Well, you were a very *convincing* escaped patient when you dashed into the reception area like that,' Celia MacDonald commented with a broad smile of her own. 'In fact, I think it might be an idea if you were to tidy yourself up a wee bit before you go back out there or they might wonder about the calibre of the staff working at St Augustine's these days.'

Wolff glanced down at his clothes and blinked, and they all noticed for the first time since the youngster had almost disembowelled himself just how disordered he was still looking, with his tie at half-mast and his shirt-tail still hanging out of the waistband of his dark trousers.

'It's not my fault,' he said as he looked around the room, his expression as innocent as a choirboy's until he flicked a quick glance in Laura's direction.

She had a sudden sinking feeling that she wasn't going to like what was coming next.

'You should have seen Sister Kirkland!' he continued in tones of bitter complaint. 'She was like a wild woman, wrenching at my clothes as if she couldn't wait to get me out of them!'

For one horrible moment Laura thought she was going to die of embarrassment and then she was afraid she wasn't, but in the end she decided that retaliation would be far more satisfying than either option.

'Well, you *are* the newest doctor in the department and we haven't had any fresh meat for a while,' she commented, her own brand of apparently accidental innuendo garnering another round of laughter which finally dispelled the air of tension which had been hanging over the department.

'So you're after fresh meat, are you?' Wolff murmured in her ear as he followed her out of the room, and Laura cursed the fact that she hadn't moved faster to avoid the possibility that he would continue to make her the focus of his wicked taunts.

'Not personally,' she said, pleased to note that her voice was calmly dismissive.

He was silent for a moment as he paced along beside her and, while she was all too conscious of the fact that he kept glancing towards her, she could almost hear his brain working.

'Do you mind if I ask you a question?' he ventured at last, and the very hesitancy of his tone made her pause to look all the way up at his puzzled expression.

She shrugged, giving him tacit permission.

'Are you a lesbian?'

He asked the question very softly but, as far as Laura was concerned, it felt almost like a shouted accusation.

'No!' she gasped, her shock at the unexpectedness of it robbing her of further speech.

'So why the strange "blow hot, blow cold" attitude towards men? Do you brush us all off the same way?'

For several seconds Laura felt quite sick that somehow she had apparently betrayed the raw hurt she carried inside. She'd always thought that she managed to keep her emotions under fairly good control, but Wolff Bergen seemed to have picked up instantly on the distance she preferred to keep between herself and any man.

There was one brief moment when she thought she was going to be overwhelmed by the memories of her betrayal and for just an instant she imagined what it might be like to pour all the agony out, but then anger roared in to rebuild her shattered defences and she turned on him.

'Oh, I'm so sorry,' she said in a voice positively dripping with sweetness, 'I didn't realise that it might hurt your ego not to have *all* the nurses at your feet.'

He didn't reply, but she witnessed the way the muscles

in his jaw tightened when he clenched his teeth.

The silence began to feel as if it were stretching into infinity when he finally broke it.

'A bad relationship?' he suggested, almost too gently, and Laura felt the sudden pressure of scalding tears behind her eyes at the accuracy of his insight.

'Dr Bergen. . .?'

Before Laura could confirm or deny his theory there was an imperative call in a clipped Scottish accent.

'Yes, Sister?' he replied, without breaking eye contact with Laura.

'There's a child arriving in just a matter of minutes. He fell out of a window onto a garden cane and impaled himself.'

'Warn Theatre and get the blood bank to stand by,' Wolff directed, his mind instantly firing on all cylinders. 'Which room is clear?'

'Two, and John Preece is calling Alex Marshall so they'll be on standby,' Celia informed him before she turned away smartly.

With those words, Laura realised that to save time her superior had already contacted the duty anaesthetist and her favourite orthopaedic surgeon.

For just a moment she was overwhelmed by the sheer volume of knowledge and experience she would need to amass before she was ready to take on a post as senior as Sister MacDonald's and then she, too, switched onto automatic pilot and hurried towards emergency room two.

By the time the banshee wail of the ambulance was heard outside the doors she'd double-checked all the supplies they might need and the room was ready for action.

'Vital signs all apparently normal,' were the first words

she heard as Ted Larrabee's opposite number, Mike Wilson, wheeled the trolley through. 'This is Simon. He's seven.'

'Hello, Simon. I'm Laura,' she said in a soothing voice as she leant towards him, trying to reassure him with a gentle squeeze when she held his limp hand.

Huge blue eyes looked up at her in open terror over the clear plastic Entonox mask, tears sliding silently out of the corners and into the soft spikes of his tough-kid haircut.

'You'll have to stay very still until we find out where you hurt yourself, OK?'

He tried to nod, but was prevented by the collar protecting his neck until he could be checked for fractures.

The radiographer called a warning and Laura released his hand to step back while the first shot was taken, her eyes riveted by the sight of the blood-stained stick angled up through the centre of his chest.

The injury was so near so many vital organs—his heart and lungs, as well as the major arteries supplying them and the rest of his body. And this was totally separate from the fact that the fall alone could have caused terrible skeletal damage.

As the minutes passed Laura's awful feeling of dread gradually began to lift as test after test proved negative.

'No broken neck,' Wolff confirmed when the plates went up on the view-box, 'and it looks as if the stick has passed right through, without causing any real damage to any of his vital organs.'

Laura drew in a deep breath and reached for Simon's hand again as the next round of tests began, hoping that this time a miracle had happened.

'Good boy,' she murmured as she smiled down at

him again. 'You're staying nice and still for us.'

She'd been holding his little grubby paw for comfort and, when she had to move out of the way to allow Wolff to move closer, released her hold on his hand and gave his foot a little squeeze instead before she moved aside.

Knowing how ticklish children tended to be, she was surprised when he didn't react to the pressure, and a nasty bell began to ring at the back of her mind.

Before she could voice her concern Wolff had begun his neurological screening test by drawing the pointed handle of his reflex hammer along the sole of Simon's foot.

There was no reaction and, suddenly, instead of the light sound of relief in the talk around the table there was an ominous silence.

Laura met Wolff's shadowed eyes as he straightened up briefly beside Simon on the other side of the trolley, and without a word being spoken she knew that he shared her fears.

'Simon? I'm Dr Bergen,' he said as he leant towards the young lad with a gentle smile. 'Can you help me do some tests?'

'Yes,' he whispered, and Laura's heart went out to him. He was trying to be so brave and, if her suspicious were correct, he was going to need every ounce of courage he possessed.

'What I'm going to do is touch your skin in different places,' Wolff explained. 'I want you to tell me when you can feel my touch so I know which bits you've hurt. OK?'

'OK,' he whispered.

He'd stopped crying now, but the silvery tracks were still visible on his pale skin.

Systematically Wolff moved his hands backwards and

forwards and up and down the child's limbs, and while
Laura heard Simon whisper a quiet 'Yes' whenever his
arms and chest were touched there was a heart-rending
silence when the contact moved below mid-chest level.

'That's all for now, Simon. Thank you for helping me.'
Wolff smiled again as he reached out a hand to ruffle the
silky hedgehog strands of blond hair.

'Doctor?' The youngster paused and swallowed, his chin
wobbling as he gathered his words. 'Do. . .do my mum
and dad know where I am?'

'Yes, Simon, they know. They're waiting outside.'

'Can. . .can I see them?' he asked hesitantly. 'Is. . .is
Mum really mad at me?'

'Of course you can see them, Simon, but it will only be
for a few minutes because then we'll be putting you to
sleep so we can take the stick away.'

'Oh. . .OK. . . But before they come in. . .' he glanced
pleadingly from Laura to Wolff and back again '. . .will
you tell her I'm sorry for opening the window?'

'I'll tell her,' Wolff promised with a smile, but Laura
realised that it didn't quite reach his eyes.

As he stripped off his disposables and left the room she
began to coil the various IVs and monitor leads neatly
around Simon's still form as she began to prepare him for
transfer up to Theatre.

She knew that the desolate expression she had witnessed
in Wolff's eyes meant that he was already trying to find
the words to tell Simon's parents the bad news—that it
looked as if the stick that their son had fallen on had missed
all his internal organs, only to sever his spinal cord.

*   *   *

It was nearly half an hour before she saw Wolff again, and he looked as if he'd aged ten years in the interim.

'Have you got time for a coffee?' Laura offered, beckoning him towards the kitchenette. She'd heard the kettle whistle not long ago and it seemed like hours since she'd last had time for a drink.

Wolff probably hadn't stopped for one either and, by the look of him, he needed it more than she did.

He propped himself silently into the corner formed by the two work-surfaces and watched silently while she spooned granules into two mugs and topped them up.

Laura handed him one of them and waited while he took his first couple of sips before she spoke.

'How is he?' she asked, knowing that she wouldn't have to say who she was talking about.

He closed his eyes and shook his head.

'Apparently there's an outside chance that the damage to his spinal cord isn't total, or might be temporary, but. . .' He shook his head again, sighing deeply before he raised sombre eyes to meet hers. 'That's what I had to tell his parents so I didn't take away all hope but, if I'm honest with myself, I'd have to say that it's pretty certain that he'll be paralysed from mid-chest downwards.'

'And if that happens he'll lose control of all bodily functions below that point, too,' Laura said, confirming what they both knew to be the almost inevitable outcome, and she dragged her eyes away to stare silently down into the steam wafting up from the mug.

'It just seems so bloody unfair,' Wolff suddenly muttered, his delivery of the words almost vicious. 'He's only seven years old, for heaven's sake!'

Laura knew what he meant.

Her thoughts had been running along similar lines ever since she'd realised the probable extent of young Simon's injuries. It didn't matter that she was seeing the results of accidents and illness all day long—it was the children who touched her heart.

She'd watched Simon's mother when she'd seen her son lying helpless on the trolley, the garden cane still sticking up grotesquely out of his chest, and had marvelled at her control.

How had the poor woman managed to stay so calm and brave while she'd stroked his forehead and reassured him that she wasn't really cross with him for opening his bedroom window?

How had she managed to stop herself from screaming aloud at the devastation that one bout of childish disobedience had made of his life?

How would *she* have coped if it had been *her* precious child lying on that trolley instead. . .?

But it wasn't her child because she didn't have a child, and it was about time she resigned herself to the fact that it was unlikely that she ever would. . .

'Thanks,' Wolff murmured, breaking into the misery of her wandering thoughts. 'I needed that. . .and the company.'

'You're welcome,' she said, realising that he seemed to have lowered some sort of defensive screen. For the first time she felt as if she was seeing the real man rather than the ever-alert, tightly controlled doctor she usually saw.

In spite of the coffee, he still looked far too weary and there were several hours yet before he could sign off and go home.

'Any idea what's waiting for us out there?' he said as

he reached across and rinsed out his mug under the tap.

'Last time I looked there were three assorted chest complaints, two lacerations waiting for stitches. . .'

'And a partridge in a pear tree,' he finished with a sigh and an attempt at a smile. 'Well, let's get going and see how fast we can get rid of them before the next few verses arrive!'

They were doing well until they came to the first of the lacerations and found an elderly military gentleman cradling a blood-soaked dressing round one hand.

Even then, it wasn't his injury that caused the problem.

He began by describing how he'd gashed his hand when he'd tried to prise the top off a tin of paint with a screwdriver which had slipped.

After that, his sole topic of conversation had been the earlier disturbance with the young knife-wielding thug.

'They all know their rights, you know,' he pontificated, wincing as Wolff injected around the edges of the wound to deaden feeling, ready for cleaning and stitching. 'They all know what they're entitled to from the rest of society, but how many of them bother fulfilling their responsibilities towards that same society?'

Wolff flicked a glance towards Laura and raised one eyebrow. For the sake of their verbose patient he made a noncommittal noise as he concentrated on trimming the ragged edges of the gash, but as a response it was obviously enough to persuade his patient that he had a willing audience.

'They've had it too easy all their lives, that's what's wrong with them—free medicine, free schooling, cash handouts so they can spend it on drugs and trail round the countryside like rent-a-mob to cause the maximum disruption to other law-abiding people.

'Ah, but,' he continued, barely taking the time to draw a breath, 'just look what happens when you suggest that they get off their lazy backsides and look for a job to *earn* their living! They lift their hands up in horror and say you're encroaching on their precious rights! Pah!'

He fixed Laura with a baleful gaze.

'Do you know, sometimes I think it would be a damn good idea to flood the whole country with a batch of bad drugs and wipe the whole lot of them out. Bloody parasites. . . Ow!'

'I'm sorry, sir, did I hurt you?' Wolff asked, obviously surprised because he'd already got halfway through the job of stitching the gash up without any problem.

'No, no, Doctor. You carry on. I'll be all right,' the dapper gentleman assured him, studiously avoiding looking at his injured hand.

'I can put some more local anaesthetic in if you need it,' Wolff offered, reaching out one gloved hand for the syringe on the tray beside him. 'There's no need for you to suffer.'

'No, thank you, Doctor,' he said courteously, and Laura saw a slight hint of heightened colour in his leathery cheeks. 'Actually, I hate to have to admit it but I can't stand injections of any kind so if you can put up with me sounding off while I take my own mind off what you're doing. . .?'

Wolff nodded his understanding. 'Feel free, if it helps you to cope with it,' he invited. 'From what I can gather, there are a fair number of people who would agree with every word you've said.'

'And they're probably the ones who do a fair day's work for a fair day's pay and can't stand the injustice of those who milk the system without ever having contributed towards it,' their patient replied, back in full flow again.

'I hope I'm not on duty when he needs those taking out again,' Laura joked as she rubbed her ears. 'I now know what the expression "an ear-bashing" means—I wonder if that's how he copes with all the problems in his life?'

'I thought it was women who were supposed to talk their problems to death?' Wolff said, poker-faced, as he completed his notes.

'Some doctors think that's why women live longer than men—because they take the edge off their problems by talking about them,' Laura pointed out. 'And no jokes about it just *seeming* longer,' she added hurriedly when she saw the start of a sly smile on his face.

'As if I would!' he countered, then grew serious again. 'I sometimes wonder. . .' He shook his head.

'Wonder what?' Laura prompted, an intuitive feeling telling her that it was important to get him to complete the thought.

'Whether talking about a problem really *would* make things more bearable or whether it would just keep dragging it up again, like picking the scab off a wound instead of letting it heal in peace.'

Laura was surprised at the depth of thought Wolff had obviously given the idea. Perhaps he, too, had had bad experiences he was trying to cope with. She was still trying to decide what to say when Leo's voice intruded on them.

'Hey, how's it going?' he demanded jovially as he

almost bounced into the tiny room and slapped his old
friend on the back. 'Is everyone taking good care of the
new boy or have you started as you mean to go on and
terrorised the lot of them straight away?'

CHAPTER FOUR

LAURA could have cursed when Leo interrupted her quiet conversation with Wolff. Then, when Hannah arrived almost on his heels, she had to resign herself to the fact that the opportunity to find out more about this intriguing man was gone—at least for the time being.

'Hey! What's this I've been hearing about the two of you rescuing the hospital from sabre-wielding terrorists?' Hannah demanded. 'I turn my back for a minute and you turn into heroes!'

'Rubbish!' Laura muttered. 'You know better than most how everything gets exaggerated in a hospital.'

She was looking at Hannah as she turned towards Wolff and saw the way her eyes widened in appreciation. She'd watched him on the stage last night—as had everyone else at the Ball—but this was obviously the first time she'd seen him in his freshly barbered doctor persona.

'Well, I can understand why you two are such good friends,' Hannah said with a grin Laura knew of old as she waved a hand towards Leo and Wolff, standing side by side. 'It's because you look so pretty beside each other!'

There were several seconds of startled silence before Leo objected heatedly.

'Pretty? Pretty?' he demanded, his strange golden eyes shooting sparks. 'I'll have you know. . .'

'Thank you kindly for the compliment,' Wolff interrupted, his slightly husky voice filled with laughter as he sketched a bow in Hannah's direction. 'It certainly scores highly for novelty value!'

Laura found it hard to agree with Hannah's description. It was true that the the two of them complemented each other, Leo's golden good looks and ready smile a perfect foil for Wolff's lean, dark and dangerous handsomeness, but she'd never have chosen such an insipid word as pretty.

Her eyes went thoughtfully from one to the other and she realised that she could imagine a good friendship developing between herself and Leo, but with Wolff. . .

She looked back at him and their eyes met, the icy blue of his cool and analytical.

There was a questioning expression in them, as if he knew that she was thinking about him and wondered what conclusions she had reached.

It was strangely difficult to drag her eyes away, as if she was forming some sort of elemental bond with him— a strange awareness that she'd never felt until she'd met his eyes for the first time last night—and she found herself shivering slightly in spite of the more than adequate heating.

Then, as if something equally elemental had told him of her new vulnerability, she saw his expression change. There was an intensity in his gaze that hadn't been there before, and she realised with a fresh shiver that the wolf he'd been named for had woken and that he was hungry and ready to prowl.

'Well,' Leo's hearty voice broke in on the strange intensity of their connection and Laura found herself dragging in a shaky breath, almost as if she'd forgotten to breathe while her gaze was held by his.

'You two weren't there to hear the announcement, but

staff at that do last night, and you know as well as I do
what a closed shop the medical world is.

'We have to behave according to the perceptions of the
outside world when we go outside our milieu, but when
we're among our colleagues we actually get the chance to
let our hair down without worrying that someone is going
to turn round and say, "But you're a *nurse!*" in a scandal-
ised tone if we get a bit tipsy or tell a risqué joke.'

Laura subsided. She had to admit that, within certain
boundaries, Hannah was right. It was just that *she* had
never been in that position before and it had left her feeling
strangely vulnerable—especially when she was overwhelmed by the memory of her reaction to Wolff's kiss
and realised that it had been watched by several hundred
pairs of eyes!

'I wish you'd warned me,' she murmured as she fought
the heat rising in her cheeks. 'It was such a shock. One
minute I was getting ready to come back here and collapse
into bed and the next I'd been manhandled up onto that
stage and. . .'

'And looked as if you were ready to come back here
and collapse into bed. . .with him!' Hannah completed.
'Wow! What a kiss! Was it as good as it looked?'

Laura glanced down at her watch in an attempt at buying
time, but her brain was whirling. She had to find something
to say to defuse Hannah's interest or she'd never hear the
end of it.

'Oh, good,' she said calmly as she forced herself to meet
her friend's eyes as if her heart weren't galloping out of
control just at the memory of that kiss. 'Wolff and I hoped
that the audience would feel that they'd had their money's
worth when we planned it.'

we did it!' Leo continued triumphantly. 'We reached the target last night!'

For a second Laura wasn't certain what he was talking about until she remembered the whole purpose of the fund-raising event.

'Well done,' she congratulated him distractedly, managing to drag a polite smile up from somewhere.

How could she concentrate on the figures he was quoting, good as they were, when she was still trembling inside from the unexpected intensity of her feelings towards his friend, standing so silent and motionless beside him.

She'd never felt like this before, not even two years ago when she had been preparing to announce her engagement to the man she'd wanted to marry. . .

Suddenly, with a sickening jolt, she remembered the reason why the engagement hadn't gone ahead. . .why she wasn't married. . .why she'd moved to St Augustine's. . . and why she'd realised that it was pointless for her even to think about taking part in the timeless mating rituals of advance and retreat.

There would be no mate for her, no happy-ever-after of marriage and family.

Two years ago she had realised that there was nothing for her to look forward to but her career, and she'd turned her attention on it with single-minded intensity.

Oh, she'd made a few adjustments, such as the change from Paediatrics to A and E, but as far as the rest was concerned everything was going well, with the next step up to Sister due soon and then. . .

'Laura?' Hannah's voice reached her, her tone making it clear that it wasn't the first time she'd spoken. 'Are you all right? You seem a bit distracted.'

'Sorry, Hannah,' she apologised, belatedly aware that Leo and Wolff must have left the room while she'd been lost in her memories. 'It's been a bit busy this morning and I'm still tired after the late night last night.' She stopped, silently cursing herself for bringing the topic up then sternly berating herself for wanting to avoid it. It was Hannah who had dumped her into the situation without warning, Hannah who had some explaining to do.

'Speaking of last night,' she began with a militant tone in her voice.

'Do you know, when I got my first look at Wolff I almost regretted giving you first go,' Hannah began in a teasing rush, carefully keeping her voice down to a confidential level.

'Especially now I've had a better look at him in daylight! Leo told me he was an old colleague so I expected someone just like him—you know, light and harmless, the typical carefree bachelor having far too much fun with far too many women to think about settling down—but *he's* rather delicious, isn't he?'

Laura couldn't help agreeing, but she was startled by a sharp twist of jealousy when she realised that Hannah would have no reason to rebuff Wolff's advances when he decided that Laura's unwillingness wasn't worth the effort to break down.

'That's neither here nor there,' Laura said as she banished the familiar little grey cloud to the darkest corner of her heart.

Determination lifted her chin as she fixed Hannah with a stern gaze. 'You persuaded me to go the Ball on the pretext that it would be a good way to meet my new colleagues, and then you pull a stunt like that! What on

earth possessed you to set me up like that? Was it d
ate? Was that why you wanted me to go?'

Hannah obviously heard the hurt in her voice, wl
she'd tried so hard to hide, and she reacted instantly.

'No, Laura!' She sounded stricken, one hand reachin
out to cover Laura's clenched fist. 'It wasn't like that, i
promise you.'

'Well, then, what *was* it like? Why *did* you do it?'

'Because I thought it would be a harmless bit of fun,
and I thought you would enjoy it,' Hannah said earnestly,
her dark blue eyes utterly guileless. 'I know you've never
been much of a one for making an exhibition of yourself
but you've seemed so. . .so subdued since you arrived and
I thought it might cheer you up.'

'Cheer me up?' Laura questioned heatedly, finding it
difficult to remember to keep her voice down. 'You thought
it would cheer me up to make a spectacle of myself in
front of everyone? I rather thought that when you started
a new job the idea was to make a good impression!'

'In your work, yes,' Hannah agreed. 'And, if what I'y
been hearing over the last couple of days is anything
go by, you've already *made* a good impression.'

She held her hand up when Laura tried to interru
obviously determined to have her say.

'Look, Laura, I don't know what happened to you a
I moved away, and I won't pry. You can tell me as m
or as little as you want to in your own time. But you r
know that I wouldn't willingly do anything to jeopar
your career.'

'But. . .' Laura began.

'Anyway,' her friend continued as if she hadn't
noticed the attempted interruption, 'it was St Augus

The way Hannah's face fell was so comical that Laura almost apologised for spoiling her illusions.

'You planned it?' she squeaked in disbelief. 'When? You only met him when Leo helped you up onto the stage.'

'While we were dancing,' Laura elaborated, making sure she kept the story simple. 'You must have seen us talking?'

'Well, yes...but I thought he must have been saying something...' She shrugged, obviously disappointed.

'As far as I remember, it was something like, "Here we go," or "Hold tight," before he did the deed,' Laura said, keeping her crossed fingers out of sight. 'And, considering the fact that we were both dragooned into it, I think you and Leo got a better deal than you deserved.'

'But I only...'

'Now—' Laura continued quickly with an ostentatious look at her watch '—I've stood chatting quite long enough so I'm going back to work.' She swished past her friend and out into the corridor, making her escape before Hannah could get her second wind.

The last part of her shift was relatively uneventful, especially when compared to the turmoil of the earlier half.

She was surprised not to see Wolff about—according to the board his spell of duty was due to end at the same time as hers—and then silently scolded herself for even noticing.

Her last port of call at the end of her shift was the staffroom, where she intended to collapse in a heap with a cup of coffee before she went out into the cold and dark of the night for the walk back to her room.

Unless Hannah called in before she went home to her tiny flatlet, or one of her new neighbours knocked on her door to speak to her while she finally forced herself to finish her unpacking, this would be her last chance for a bit of company before she came back on duty tomorrow.

She pushed open the door and paused, surprised to find the room deserted and most of the lights turned off.

Mildly disappointed, she'd just decided that she might as well grab her belongings and go back to her room for the longed-for coffee while she started the dreaded chore when a strange sound drew her attention towards the furthest shadowy corner of the room.

There was someone there, slumped in the corner of a two-seater settee with his head twisted at such an awkward angle that he must have fallen asleep unexpectedly.

As she watched his whole body twitched—almost as if he were trying to fight an invisible enemy—and he made the same strangled moaning sound deep in his throat which had first attracted her attention.

She hovered in the doorway, not quite certain what to do.

If it was a junior doctor, taking advantage of a lull in his duties to grab a few minutes of sleep, he wouldn't be very pleased if she woke him up to ask if he was all right.

On the other hand, if it was someone in pain, or. . .

Her train of thought was completely derailed when the shadowy figure moved again and the meagre light caught the newly familiar shape of Wolff's face.

Involuntarily she found herself walking towards him, a frown pleating her forehead as she tried to see what was the matter with him. Was he unwell or. . .?

'No. . . Don't. . . Please. . .'

His husky voice was roughened still further by sleep and now that she was closer she could see that he was in the throes of an awful dream.

'Please. . .don't die. . .'

There was such an awful emptiness in his voice that Laura couldn't help reaching out towards him in sympathy. His cheek felt so hot against her cool hand that it almost seared her, and as he moved convulsively in the throes of the nightmare his jaw rasped audibly against the soft skin of her palm.

'Wolff?' she murmured, bending forward to call him out of the nightmare. 'Wolff, can you hear me?'

She could tell when he woke up as his whole body seemed to grow tense from the electric point of contact with her hand, as though he was prepared for some kind of blow. Then the dark crescents of his lashes rose and she was captured in the stunning clarity of his blue eyes.

He blinked up at her, clearly disorientated, and she snatched her hand away, feeling almost guilty for invading his privacy.

'Laura?' His voice was a deep rumble and seemed to reverberate inside her chest long after it had left his. 'What. . .what's the matter? Am I needed on duty?'

He started to struggle upright on the seat, the effort clearly a major effort, and she stepped back to allow him more space.

'No. It's all right. You're off duty now, but you'd fallen asleep and. . .' She paused, not quite knowing what to say.

'Oh. . .'

It seemed that she didn't need to say any more as he rubbed the palms of both hands over his face.

'Was I shouting?' he asked quietly as he took his hands away and looked up at her. 'Sometimes. . .'

'No,' she hastened to reassure him. 'More of a mutter, and I wouldn't have heard that much except for the fact that I came in for a cup of coffee.'

He sighed deeply and rested his head back against the nubbly upholstery.

'I suppose I should be grateful for small mercies,' he said quietly. 'Poor Leo hasn't been quite so lucky. I think he's beginning to regret letting me stay.'

'Why?'

'Because he's hardly had any sleep since I arrived.'

Laura nodded her understanding. Her eyes had grown used to the low level of lighting and when she saw the shadows like bruises under his eyes and the tension around his jaw she chanced a question.

'I take it this is a relatively new problem?'

For nearly a minute she thought that he wasn't going to answer, and was beginning to feel embarrassed at her temerity in asking something so personal.

They might have 'met' on the stage last night but, in actual fact, their acquaintance was far too new for him to. . .

'Three months,' he said baldly, staring down at the linked hands hanging between his knees. He'd propped his elbows on his thighs, as though he needed them to help him remain upright, but now the slump of his shoulders just looked defeated. 'Nearly four, all told.'

Laura was silent, trying to work out the significance of the timing without having to ask.

He looked up at her and obviously saw the puzzlement on her face.

'I volunteered for a stint in a refugee camp—just a month, initially, to give one of the other medics a break.'

He mentioned the country, and Laura's eyes widened.

There had been so much in the news over the last couple of years about the atrocities committed in that region, including horrific attempts at wholesale genocide. She had never realised that people like Wolff were on the ground there, trying to take care of the people.

'It's a living nightmare,' he said hoarsely, as if the words were forcing their way out of him whether he wanted them to or not. 'During the summer it was so hot and dry that people were dropping like flies because of dehydration, dysentery. . .you name it and we had it. It's so overcrowded that there's no way of regulating sanitation and hygiene successfully.'

He drew in a shuddering breath, as though he were drawing in strength to continue.

'It felt as if we were starting to get things a bit better organised, and I volunteered to stay on to see the job through.' His laugh was short and harsh and directed at himself.

'Then the autumn rains came, and when the temperature began to drop and the winds started blowing it wasn't long before they started dying of hypothermia. . . Then the bastards started shooting at them. . .men, women, little children. . .they didn't care. . .'

He shook his head, an expression of utter desperation on his face as he looked up at her with eyes full of unspeakable memories before he looked away—his gaze once more fixed on his knotted fingers.

She longed to be able to step forward and take him in her arms to give him some measure of comfort, but she didn't have the right.

All she could do was offer him some space while he gathered his composure so she turned towards the kettle in the corner.

'I was just going to make myself a coffee before I went

back to my room. Decaffeinated. Would you like one?'

'Ah, Laura, I think I've got beyond that.' He laughed wryly. 'I've tried staying awake to stop me dreaming about it and I've tried various ways of knocking myself out, starting with hot milky drinks right up through alcohol and drugs.'

'Not together!' Laura exclaimed in horror, wondering just how terrible his memories were that he would think of taking such chances.

'I might be desperate for a good night's sleep but I'm not terminally stupid,' he replied shortly.

'I'm sorry. I didn't mean to suggest. . .'

'No,' he interrupted with a grimace as he straightened up out of his seat, '*I'm* sorry for jumping down your throat. It was probably a reasonable question, given the way I look at the moment. Can we blame exhaustion for my lack of equanimity?'

The kettle began to hiss and Laura turned away from the all-too-attractive sight of a sleepily rumpled Wolff Bergen to reach for two mugs.

'Black?' she asked as she twisted the lid off the coffee granules.

'Actually, I think I'll go back to Leo's place, if you don't mind. Perhaps I'll be able to get some sleep before he finishes his shift, then it won't matter so much if I have to stay awake to give him a chance to sleep.'

'Good idea.' Laura smiled as she screwed the lid back on the jar again, deliberately ignoring the swift stab of disappointment that their time together was over so quickly.

She watched silently as he patted his pockets until he heard the jingle of keys and smiled in answer to his tired grin of victory.

'Well, we'll probably see each other at some stage tomorrow,' he said as he reached the door, then he paused and turned back to her, the lean planes of his face highlighted by the brighter light streaming in over him from the corridor.

He gazed at her wordlessly for a moment, as if he was trying to find words, then smiled at her, his teeth impossibly white against the dark tan of his face and his expression impossibly gentle.

'Laura. . .thanks for listening. You'll never know how much talking about it has helped.' He drew in a slow breath and straightened his shoulders. 'You never know, I might even be able to get some sleep.'

'I hope so,' Laura said, her voice a little shaky with her reaction to the events of the last few minutes. 'Goodnight, Wolff.'

She watched him pull the door open wider and answered his brief salute as he left the room.

'Sleep well,' she whispered as she heard his footsteps recede along the corridor.

She finally slid down under the covers about an hour later with a glow of satisfaction at a job well done.

As she reached up to turn off the bedside light she cast one last look around the room and saw the few knick-knacks she'd collected, displayed on the dresser and window-sill, and knew that she'd done all she could to make her temporary abode welcoming.

At least now she wouldn't feel as if she was living out of a suitcase, and she could take her time about looking for accommodation further away from the hospital when she was ready. Hannah had promised to keep her ears open but there was no rush, especially when she was intending to stay at St Augustine's for the forseeable future.

With a soft click the room was plunged into darkness and she closed her eyes with a grateful sigh, welcoming the oblivion which was never long in coming. . .only this time, her brain didn't seem to want to switch off.

Hardly surprising, she snorted softly, when she thought about all the things that had happened since she arrived.

But even as she began to make a mental list of all the events which had bombarded her it was the face of one man which filled her mental vision.

Dr Wolff Bergen.

What was it about the man that she felt such a sense of connection?

For two years she'd had no difficulty keeping men at arm's length because she'd been all but unaware of them as anything other than colleagues at work. But there was something about Wolff Bergen. . .something special which had enabled him to break effortlessly through the wall she'd built around her emotions.

For two years she'd been able to live and work without letting anything touch her too deeply, but when she'd listened to his brief account of the last three months of his life she'd been unable to prevent herself from feeling the pain she heard in his voice.

And it wasn't just Wolff Bergen, the caring doctor, who affected her, nor the fact that he had the lean grace and power of the wild animal he was named for. . . It wasn't even the fact that he danced better than Patrick Swayze. . .

Her cheeks grew warm in the darkness when she remembered how it had felt to be held so close to his body that they had seemed to become part of each other, swaying in complete harmony as if the dance had been a vertical prelude to a more ancient horizontal dance. . .

Shocked by the suddenly explicit pictures flooding her brain, she opened her eyes wide and stared up at the plain white ceiling above her bed. She was horribly conscious of the fact that her pulse was galloping at the base of her throat and her ragged breathing was causing an exquisite friction between her tightly furled nipples and the soft knitted fabric of the oversized T-shirt she wore to bed.

That was just a sample of the chaos which Wolff was causing in her life.

It was a long time since she'd allowed herself to think and feel like a woman, and in the space of twenty-four hours the man had managed to make her all too aware of her feminine side.

She flounced over in the bed and thumped her pillow, wondering if he was having any more luck than she was at falling asleep, before she determinedly banished him from her thoughts.

Tomorrow was soon enough to let the dratted man into her head again. Tonight she needed to sleep or she'd never be able do do her job properly.

A quick glance at the board when she scooted past on her way to get rid of her damp parka gave Laura the unwelcome news that Wolff was starting his shift at the same time as she was, and she groaned silently to herself.

If she hadn't known that the rotas were worked out in advance she would almost have suspected Hannah of engineering the amount of time she and Wolff seemed to have spent together since he'd arrived.

She'd be glad when Nick Prince and his bride returned

from their honeymoon. At least it would mean that there was one less chance that she'd be rostered at the same time as Wolff.

It wasn't that he was a bad doctor, she mused as she tried to calm a hysterical woman. On the contrary, the way he was dealing with the severe asthma attack from which the woman's four-year-old son was suffering was ample evidence that he was very good.

Almost as soon as the mother had run into the department with the youngster in her arms Wolff had recognised the symptoms, grabbed an oxygen mask and slipped the elastic over the back of the child's head to hold it in position.

'Nebuliser,' he rapped out urgently while he was checking the child's abnormally slow pulse and his almost non-existent breathing.

Laura was already reaching for the unit, knowing that he was going to need it to administer the life-saving drugs directly into the child's lungs like an aerosol. Only then would the dangerous spasms be released so that the boy could draw in the air he needed.

'Connect the unit to oxygen rather than compressed air,' Wolff directed as he added the correct quantity of bronchodilator to the normal saline in the compact machine and set the delivery rate.

While he was busy with that Laura was able to tape a butterfly needle in position on the back of the little chubby hand, and by the time Wolff straightened up from his task the microdrip administration set was ready to begin IV rehydration.

For all the severity of the child's condition on arrival, it wasn't long before the drug regimen had started to take effect.

'Right, Staff, if you can give a ring up to the children's ward and warn them that we've got a customer for them,' Wolff began, only to be interrupted by the child's mother.

'You're keeping him here?' she said with renewed fear in her voice. 'What's happening? Is he getting worse?'

'Not at all,' Wolff soothed with a smile. 'He's doing very well.'

'Well, why does he need to stay, then? Why can't I take him home?'

'I'd like him to stay for a little while for observation— just to make sure the drugs have done the job. If all goes well you'll probably be able to take him home later today.'

'But I'm supposed to be going to work later. . .I can't afford to wait.'

Laura was struck by the woman's apparently callous words. She'd been watching the way the mother's eyes had followed every move they'd made in their efforts to help her son and she'd been convinced that she really cared for him, but just now she'd sounded as if he was the least of her concerns.

If Laura hadn't been watching her so closely she wouldn't have seen the way her skin had paled and the way the expression in her eyes made her look like a trapped animal.

'Is there no one else to stay with your little boy while you go to work?' she asked gently, leading her a little way away from the youngster so that she would feel more comfortable about talking.

'There's only Mum, and she can't manage to look after him for long—she's waiting to have a hip replacement. She usually comes in to listen for him when he's asleep.'

'What about taking a day off work?' Wolff suggested,

but almost before he'd finished speaking the young woman was shaking her head.

'Can't,' she said bluntly. 'If I miss one more day of work I'll lose my job, and there's only me to look after Toby. His dad did a runner as soon as he knew I was pregnant.'

'Well, we'll have to see if we can sort something out with the children's ward,' Wolff said, his frown of disgust at the absent father's behaviour slow to fade. 'Perhaps they'll be able to keep him in overnight so you can collect him when you finish work in the morning. . . It will depend on how many beds there are free. . .'

His voice faded as he led the woman away towards Sister MacDonald's office, and Laura realised that he was going to hand her into that formidable woman's capable care.

Young Toby had barely disappeared into the lift, whisking him away to the paediatric ward, when the priority message came through from the ambulance centre.

'Five injuries from a robbery in the centre of town. One passer-by shot. Cranial injury. ETA seven minutes.'

CHAPTER FIVE

'ALERT X-ray and the labs, and make sure the ventilator is ready.'

'How much O-negative blood have we got on hand until we can get him cross-matched?'

'Contact someone from Neurosurgery and warn Theatre. They may not have much time to prepare if he needs to go straight up.'

'Draw some drugs up so they're ready to go—I'll need lignocaine for premedication, etomidate for anaesthetic and succinylcholine to speed intubation. I'll sort out the doses in a minute.'

The questions and orders emerged in an almost unbroken stream as the department was readied for the arrival of the injured, and by the time the approaching siren's ululation was cut off they were waiting by the door.

The double doors at the back of the ambulance swung wide and the trolley emerged as if jet-propelled, one uniformed attendant holding up IV bags while he kept pace with the swiftly moving cortège.

'He needs to be intubated,' one of the paramedics said. 'He's breathing on his own—just—but he doesn't sound good and he's unresponsive to stimuli. There was a stray gunshot during a robbery and he had the bad luck to be in the way. The injuries on the other four are mainly from flying glass and shock.'

He was only young, Laura saw as she looked down at

the poor man, struggling to draw a ragged breath then exhaling with a strange sobbing whistle.

Just twenty-two, the paramedic confirmed, and while he was swiftly transferred from the ambulance trolley the frantically moving staff who surrounded him were very careful not to touch the side of his head covered by the blood-soaked dressing.

One pair of hands was swiftly stripping his clothing away while another was slotting X-ray cassettes into position, ready for the first shot to be taken.

A mask connected to the piped oxygen supply was held tightly over his face to try to get as much of the precious element into him as possible before he was intubated, while additional IV's were being started and a detailed examination was being made of the rest of his body for other injuries.

Laura continued to monitor the patient's pulse and respiration as the correct doses of drugs were injected to sedate and paralyse his injured body for intubation, and soon saw him become flaccid and stop breathing.

The cervical collar had been opened at the front to aid the positioning of the laryngoscope and, with an expertise which spoke of much practice, Wolff began to slide the instrument into position.

'Can't see a thing,' he muttered, and there was a brief pause to suction blood and saliva away before he could see the vocal cords and finish positioning the laryngoscope.

'Tube,' he said, one hand reaching blindly.

Laura had it in her hand, ready and waiting, and within seconds he had passed it down into the trachea.

'Oxygen,' he ordered briskly, then listened to the sounds in the young man's chest for a minute to confirm that the tube had been positioned correctly before he straightened up.

'Hyperventilate to reduce swelling of the brain,' he directed as the O-negative blood was hung and a catheter inserted to drain his bladder. Then an orogastric tube was snaked past the endotracheal tube and down into the stomach to empty out the contents.

At intervals there was the familiar sound of the X-ray machine taking another of a series of shots of the skull and neck but it happened almost without comment, all of them so familiar with the signals that they were able to remain intent upon their own tasks.

'Blood pressure's stable but his Glasgow coma scale score was very low,' Laura heard Wolff say to the neuro-surgeon as they stood in front of the X-ray view-box and he clipped the plates into position with a practised flick of the wrist.

'His whole skull is unstable—it looks as if the shock wave from the impact of the bullet has cracked it in five or six places.'

'God knows what sort of damage it's done to the brain itself, then,' Wolff's deeper voice commented.

'Quite. That's why I need to get him up to Theatre as soon as possible. I need to get a tube into the ventricles of his brain to relieve the pressure there—just in case,' his colleague replied, and they turned back towards the still, silent figure on the table.

'Just in case' his brain swelled as a result of the trauma, Laura interpreted, and, at the same time, 'just in case' he survived, in which case they didn't want to chance further brain damage from uncontrolled swelling.

Once again there was concerted activity as he was prepared for the journey upstairs, with notes, IV bags, oxygen and monitors stacked around his deathly still figure on the trolley.

Their hands moved with familiar speed and efficiency. There was no need to speak, the only sounds intruding on the edges of their concentration being the rhythmic bleep of the cardiac monitor and the suck-and-blow of the ventilator.

The room had hardly had time to be cleared of the debris when the phone rang.

'Damn.'

Wolff's muttered curse might just as well have been shouted for the impact it had on the remaining staff.

'No good?' Laura queried when he put the phone down, but the expression on his face had already told her the worst.

'He got the tube in but instead of clear cerebrospinal fluid the tube delivered chunks of brain matter.'

Laura's shoulders slumped. She knew as well as anyone in the room that this result meant that the young man's brain had been hopelessly damaged—and all because he'd been in the wrong place at the wrong time.

'Have we managed to trace any family?' Wolff asked. He was obviously thinking ahead to the task of explaining what had happened to the young man, and Laura could see the tension tightening his jaw. It was one part of his job which she would never envy.

'I'll find out,' Laura volunteered, and reached for the phone to connect her to Celia MacDonald. If anyone knew she would.

Within minutes she had the answer.

'They've contacted his parents—they're on their way

in. He was carrying a donor card and had put his name on the organ donor register.'

'Good lad,' Wolff said softly, a sad smile creasing the corners of his eyes. 'Now we've got the job of consulting his parents for confirmation that we can plan to harvest his organs but, hopefully, if he'd told them about his wishes. . .'

He stripped off his disposable apron and dumped it in the bin, then slid his arms into a fresh white coat.

'Sometimes I wonder why I chose this job,' he murmured as if he were talking to himself. 'So many of them never get a second chance.'

While Wolff talked to the bereaved parents in the small interview room Laura's work went on as she helped to take care of the other victims of the incident.

It was painstaking work to make a good job of repairing the numerous lacerations, caused by flying plate glass, and several of the cuts were very deep.

'I never was much of an oil painting,' commented one gentleman as the last of several dozen tiny stitches was put into a jagged wound down the side of his face.

'Well, once the stitches come out and the scar has had a little time to fade perhaps you'll be able to tell people it's a war wound,' Leo suggested.

'Better still, be mysterious and don't say where you got it,' Laura advised with a grin. 'Most women are a pushover for a wounded hero.'

'Really?' Their patient sounded sceptical.

'Of course,' she assured him, knowing that he really *wanted* to believe what she was telling him. 'You only have to look at the world's great literature—Jane Eyre's Mr Rochester must be one of the most famous.'

'Anyway,' Leo added, 'I've done my best to make certain that it heals neatly.'

'So I won't frighten the horses?'

'Or children and women of a sensitive disposition,' Leo confirmed with a grin as he taped a protective dressing over his handiwork. 'And if you can give yourself a vitamin boost to help your body heal quickly you'll soon be on form again.'

Laura escorted the gentleman towards the reception area and walked over to see who was next.

'One more for stitching?' she asked, and was handed the outpatient details.

Automatically she glanced down at them, read the phrase 'hit by a candelabrum' and blinked, the corners of her mouth curling up with the threat of a smile.

'Which one is he?' she enquired, hoping that her attack of humour would be under control before she had to face the man at close quarters.

'He's the one sitting round the corner out of sight,' the clerk told her in a grim mutter, not a smile in sight.

'You'll recognise him because he's the one handcuffed to the policeman.'

'Handcuffed. . .?' Laura was startled.

Suddenly she guessed who their next patient was, but that still didn't tell her how he'd come to be injured.

'A candelabrum?' she murmured, her mind boggling.

'It was a jeweller's shop he was trying to rob, and when the plate glass shattered one of the staff was quick-witted enough to grab a silver candelabrum and knock the beggar for six.'

Laura had been hoping to explain the circumstances to Leo before he was confronted by his next patient—just in case anyone made any unfortunate comments—but when she walked in it was Wolff waiting in the room.

He looked terrible, his face almost grey in spite of the deep colour he still sported from his time abroad, and his eyes had gone that empty icy colour again.

Laura's heart went out to him, especially when he saw who his next patient was. If he gritted his teeth any harder they would shatter.

She could only guess how the interview with the young man's parents had gone and, with the glowering young man in front of him being the cause of the tragedy, this was hardly the time to ask whether they'd had permission. . .

On second thoughts, she mused, remembering Wolff's anger at his feeling of helplessness in the face of the refugees' suffering, perhaps this was *exactly* the right time to ask about it.

'Did you see his parents?' she said quietly as she placed the suture tray ready. She'd already pulled a seat across so that the policeman could stay beside his charge and yet not get in the way.

Wolff was silent for a moment, a questioning expression on his face as he gazed at her. He knew that it was unlike her to talk about one patient while in the room with another, and he was obviously puzzled.

Laura flicked a glance down at the patient waiting for his attention and raised an eyebrow, knowing how quick on the uptake he usually was.

She saw the expression on his face change and he nodded briefly.

'Yes. I saw his parents,' he confirmed in an icily quiet voice as he reached for the prepared syringe and began to inject around the edges of the wound high up on the man's forehead to deaden it, ready for cleaning and stitching. 'Obviously they were devastated. He'd only told them yesterday that he was going to get engaged, and he was apparently looking at the rings in the jeweller's window.'

Laura knew from the way the policeman's head jerked towards them that he'd made the connection between their conversation and his prisoner, and the way that surly young man stiffened told them all that he'd understood, too.

'Did you ask them whether they were going to allow us to use his body for organ donation?' she asked after a brief pause.

'Yes. I asked,' he said gruffly. 'They knew that he carried a donor card but they hadn't realised—or didn't remember—that he'd filled in the form to be put on the organ donor register.'

'Did they give consent in the end?'

Her question seemed to hang in the air above their sullen patient, his pale brown eyes darting from one to the other as he waited silently for the reply.

'They did,' Wolff confirmed, then paused to position another stitch. 'The labs are doing the cross-matching and tissue-typing at the moment, and there's a computer search ready to run to match up with potential recipients.'

He snipped the thread and glanced up at Laura, totally ignoring the patient lying frozen with apprehension under the poised needle as he continued.

'Even though he's dead they're keeping his body alive on the life-support machine to keep it fresh until they get the go-ahead,' he said.

For just a second Laura wondered why Wolff was telling her something which she already knew, then she realised that he was pitching the level of his explanation so that the rest of his audience would be in no doubt about what was happening.

'If everything goes well they'll get the temperature-controlled containers ready and begin harvesting. We should be able to make use of his kidneys, his heart, his liver, his lungs, his pancreas, his corneas and maybe even some sections of his bones and strips of skin for grafting— I understand there are several programmes where they're experimenting with transplanting whole joints rather than using artificial ones.'

'My God!' croaked the man on the table under Wolff's hands, his face absolutely green with nausea as a result of their deliberately gruesome conversation. 'You're sick! You're talking about chopping him up as if you're butchers with a piece of meat!'

'Oh, no, sunshine!' Wolff said with bitter emphasis, the loathing in his icy blue eyes utterly intimidating as he bent forward again with his needle. '*We're* not the butchers... *We* didn't kill him. We're just trying to minimise the senseless waste of his life!'

The rest of the stitching was achieved in total silence, the young thug gazing up in terror at the icy disdain in Wolff's eyes as he finished the job with his usual attention to detail.

'You can take him away now,' Wolff directed the uniformed policeman as he stood up and stripped his gloves off. 'He won't need to come back here to have the stitches taken out—unless we're the closest hospital to whichever prison he's sent to.'

He glared down at the cowering lout one last time.

'All I can say to you is that while you're locked up I hope you think about some way of making your life count for something. Having killed someone, I reckon that means that you've got twice as much good to do in the world to make up for it.'

A shiver worked its way up the back of Laura's neck as she watched him stalk out of the room. She could almost feel the pain radiating from him, and if he'd been holding his spine any more rigidly it would have snapped.

For the rest of his shift he seemed very subdued, in spite of the fact that Leo had begun regaling the rest of the staff with anecdotes of the things the two of them had got up to when they'd been in medical school.

Laura took everything with a large pinch of salt, far more interested in watching Wolff's reaction to the stories than in the content of them.

One thing she noticed was that most of the tales either concerned feats of physical daring—such as the time-honoured placing of a bedpan on top of the ornamental cupola over the principal's office—or involved copious quantities of semi-naked females— such as the equally time-honoured setting-off of the fire alarm in the nurses' home at dead of night, much to the delight of the rest of the waiting camera-wielding male medical students.

While Wolff bore it all with a smile and the odd quiet disclaimer, Laura had the feeling that it was not so much equanimity which was helping him to cope with it as the fact that his thoughts were elsewhere.

She had just finished her shift and was on her way to collect her belongings before she made a quick dash out to the shops for some coffee and milk when she passed the door of the staffroom.

Several paces further along the corridor it dawned on

her that there had been someone standing in the dimly lit room, his figure faintly outlined against the window.

She paused a second then shook her head. For heaven's sake, she'd known the man for less than three days. There was no way that she could possibly recognise him from such a brief glance.

Her curiosity wouldn't let her continue on her way, though, and she found herself retracing her steps to the door and peering through the panel of safety glass.

The thump of recognition her heart gave was confirmation enough and, almost without realising that she'd done it, she saw her hand come up to push the door open and then she was walking in.

He was so still that she didn't think he'd heard her come in until his husky voice reached her, then she realised that he must have seen her reflection in the glass.

'Have you come to join me for a coffee?' he asked, and she willingly took the question as an invitation, making straight for the kettle and switching it on.

She turned to face him and realised that he hadn't moved. He was still facing the window, staring out at the dirty yellow tinge of the pseudo night sky with his hands wrapped around a mug.

'Is yours fresh or do you want a top-up?' she asked, marvelling that she had recognised him with so few clues to go on. She would almost defy a sophisticated computer to do better. . .

'Actually, I was just thinking that I don't want to be here but that I don't seem to have the energy or the inclination to move.'

Laura's heart sank into her eminently comfortable shoes with a sickening thud.

'You mean you're regretting coming to St Augustine's?' she enquired, almost holding her breath as she waited for his reply. Did this mean that as soon as Nick Prince returned he would be leaving? And why did it matter so much to her—he was just another doctor, wasn't he?

'At this precise moment, yes,' he admitted gruffly. 'But what I really meant was that I need to get out of here before the walls start closing in on me.'

'In which case,' Laura began as she reached across and switched off the kettle before it could come to the boil, 'let's sneak out before anyone notices we're going. You have finished your shift, haven't you?'

'And handed over,' he confirmed, turning towards her with a slightly arrested expression on his face. 'Where do you suggest we go?'

'Well, *I'm* going to that little corner shop in the side road behind the hospital. I need to get some milk and some coffee or I won't be able to get my eyes open tomorrow.'

She let the words die away while she waited to see what he would say.

Part of her wanted to invite him to come with her—to walk to the shop and then accompany her to her room to drink a cup of the coffee she was buying—but the habits of two years were hard to break. She couldn't afford to let anybody get too close—it hurt too much when they left. . .

'Would you mind having some company?' he asked, his tone unexpectedly hesitant. 'I don't usually let it get to me, but after that young man with the bullet. . .'

She'd had a feeling that his mood was somehow connected with that particular patient, out of all the ones he'd seen today, and that it was also connected to the things he'd seen while he'd been volunteering his time and expertise at the refugee camp.

'No problem,' she agreed easily as she turned away and began to walk towards the door, grateful that he couldn't see the idiotic grin which had just covered her face and the sudden leap in her pulse rate. 'It will be nice to have someone to talk to while I unwind.'

It was the work of seconds to grab her big puffy parka and her bag from her locker, and then they were walking out through the big automatic doors and into the dark of the November evening.

Much as Laura would have liked to prolong their time together, it was too cold to do anything but walk briskly. All too soon she had her purchases in her bag and it was time to go back to her room.

'You wouldn't. . .?'

'Could I. . .?'

They both began to speak at the same time, then both halted and laughed.

'Ladies first,' Wolff offered with an attempt at a smile, his teeth gleaming briefly in the shadows between two streetlights.

'I was only going to ask if you would like to join me for a cup of coffee,' she said, trying to sound as if his answer didn't really matter.

In actual fact, she had grown quite concerned when he'd hardly spoken during their walk. There was something weighty on his mind, and if there was any way she could help. . .

'I'd like that—in fact, that was what I was going to ask,' he said quietly, and gestured for her to walk beside him again.

The dimly lit lounge area of the nurses' accommodation was occupied by several people watching a situation comedy on the television so Laura's first choice of venue for their coffee had to be abandoned. If Wolff *did* decide that he needed to talk he wouldn't want an audience.

'We might as well drink it in my room,' Laura suggested quietly as she handed him one mug.

She turned away quickly, her cheeks glowing as she mentally crossed her fingers in the hope that they were all too engrossed in their programme to notice what was happening around them.

Still, it would be worth a little embarrassment if she could get him to relax enough to forget about whatever was playing so heavily on his mind.

She might not think it worth the price when any nurses who had noticed her disappearing towards her room with the newest and handsomest doctor on the staff started pulling her leg, but for the moment she didn't care what they thought.

By the time Laura had shut the door to her room and turned back to face Wolff he had slipped his jacket off and was standing at the foot of her bed, his mug of coffee all but forgotten as he gazed around at the small array of knick-knacks in the soft illumination of the bedside light.

'Make yourself comfortable,' she invited as she hung her own parka on the back of the door, before sitting on the edge of the only comfortable chair in the room.

Wolff took her words to heart and immediately appropriated her bed.

'Ah, bliss,' he groaned as he eased himself down onto the pile of colourful throw pillows stacked against the headboard and sprawled the rest of his long lean body bonelessly on the mattress like a lazy cat.

There was a long silence while they sipped their drinks, but it didn't feel uncomfortable. In fact, Laura was amazed just how comfortable she felt with Wolff in her room. Somehow it almost felt as if he belonged. . .

She heard him sigh deeply and her eyes were drawn to his face, unsurprised when it seemed as if he hadn't even realised that he'd made the sound—his coffee forgotten as he balanced it on his washboard-flat stomach.

Once again he was wearing that awful withdrawn expression, and she mentally crossed her fingers before she began to speak.

'Did today bring it back?' she ventured, and watched him blink while he focused on her words.

'The refugee camp? All too clearly,' he said, the corners of his mobile mouth pulling down in a grimace.

If he was surprised that she had followed his train of thought he didn't say so.

'Imagine today's event multiplied by ten, by twenty, and you'll have some idea of what it was like on a daily basis while the camp was being shelled. . .' He drew in another shuddering breath and shook his head.

'We didn't manage to save that young lad today in spite of unlimited medical supplies, personnel and all our sophisticated technology. Out there they don't stand a chance.'

Laura saw the darkness fill his eyes as the memories took over, and she couldn't remain sitting on the other side of the room with a mug in her hand as if she didn't care.

She wasn't even certain if he'd noticed when she perched on the edge of the bed beside him, but when she gently covered his clenched fist with one hand and relieved his other one of the forgotten coffee he stared at her as if he'd never seen her before.

'Ah, Laura, you can't imagine the things I saw,' he whispered, his husky voice sounding as if it was having to fight its way out through the tightness in his throat. 'You can't imagine how utterly frustrating it was to have to stand by and watch those defenceless people being systematically maimed and murdered. It didn't matter what I did—there weren't any second chances.'

He closed his eyes briefly but shook his head and opened them again as if he couldn't bear what he could see behind his eyelids.

'And every time you close your eyes you relive it all over again, especially after cases like today's,' she murmured softly, somehow knowing that it was true. 'And, gradually, because the nightmares keep waking you up you get more and more tired until you begin to feel like a rat caught in a trap with no way out.'

He gazed at her silently, and when she saw the thoughtful expression creep across his face she realised that her ready empathy had told him that she, too, was haunted by demons.

She tensed, dreading the moment when he asked her to explain—but it never came.

'Ah, Laura,' he murmured on a sigh as he wrapped one arm around her shoulders and pulled her closer.

Off balance on the squashy edge of the mattress, Laura couldn't stop herself toppling towards him and she ended up sprawled halfway across his chest.

For a moment she couldn't help the fact that the unexpected contact with the solid warmth of his body made every muscle grow tense, but when it became obvious that he only wanted to hold her for their mutual comfort she finally allowed herself to relax.

Gradually she became aware of a multitude of apparently insignificant details—such as the lingering scent of soap or aftershave she could detect on his skin, overlying his own musky warmth, and the teasing drift of his breath as it drifted over one side of her face.

His chest was broad, the fine white cotton of his shirt smooth under her cheek. Beneath the cotton there was the steady drumbeat of his heart.

When Wolff woke up it took him several seconds to work out exactly where he was, and less than one second more to decide that he liked being there.

Over the last few months it seemed as if he'd hardly spent any time settled in one place, and hardly more than a couple of nights in the same bed.

He glanced across at the bedside light and caught sight of the time shown by little alarm clock beside it with disbelief. If the glowing green figures could be believed he had just slept for seven hours without even a hint of a nightmare to disturb him.

Wolff felt a smile creep over his face as he looked down at the woman curled up beside him. The bed was so narrow that there was only room for the two of them when he held her tightly against his side, but he wasn't going to complain.

He tilted his head to get a better view of her face and marvelled at her elfin prettiness. She could only be about three or four inches above five feet, far smaller and daintier than his own six feet, but she had a strength of will and purpose big enough for an Amazon.

He frowned when he remembered the odd occasions when he'd seen hints of an enduring pain in her eyes. Last night he'd longed to ask her about her demons, had hoped that when he'd told her about his own that she would volunteer the information so that he could comfort her. . . but he could wait.

They hadn't known each other very long—he snorted softly; they didn't really know each other at all—but for the first time in his life he felt as if he'd found someone who understood how he thought and felt. . .

It was a slightly scary thought. . .almost as scary as the fact that for the first time since he'd arrived in that hell-hole of a camp he had actually slept deeply and dreamlessly, and the only reason he could see was the endearingly rumpled sprite who slept with her arms wrapped around him like a treasured teddy bear.

He looked down at her again, his eyes charting the shape of her face with its high cheek-bones, slightly pointed chin and the feathery blonde hair lying in wisps across her forehead.

Her eyelashes were several shades darker and cast fan-like shadows onto the soft peach bloom of her cheeks. And when they opened they would reveal eyes of such a dark green that the first time he'd seen them—when she'd joined him on the stage at that wretched ball—he'd thought they were black.

It wasn't until he'd turned her towards the light during that mind-boggling dance that he'd realised that they were green and all but shooting daggers at him.

He hadn't been able to resist taking advantage of the situation with that mad impulsive kiss, and he'd wondered

NO COST! NO OBLIGATION TO BUY!
NO PURCHASE NECESSARY!

PLAY "LUCKY 7"
AND GET AS MANY AS FIVE FREE GIFTS...

HOW TO PLAY:

1 With a coin, carefully scratch away the gold panel opposite. Then check the claim chart to see what we have for you – FREE BOOKS and gift – ALL YOURS! ALL FREE!

2 Send back this card and you'll receive specially selected Mills & Boon® Medical Romance™ novels. These books are yours to keep absolutely FREE.

3 There's no catch. You're under no obligation to buy anything. We charge nothing for your first shipment. And you don't have to make any minimum number of purchases – not even one!

4 The fact is thousands of readers enjoy receiving books by mail from the Reader Service™. They like the convenience of home delivery and they like getting the best new romance novels at least a month before they are available in the shops. And of course postage and packing is completely FREE!

5 We hope that after receiving your free books you'll want to remain a subscriber. But the choice is yours – to continue or cancel, any time at all! So why not take up our invitation, with no risk of any kind. You'll be glad you did!

You'll look like a million dollars when you wear this lovely necklace! Its cobra-link chain is a generous 18" long, and the beautiful puffed heart pendant will add the finishing touch to any outfit!

Play

"Lucky 7"

M7KI

Just scratch away the gold panel with a coin.
Then check below to see how many FREE GIFTS will be yours.

YES! I have scratched away the gold panel. Please send me all the gifts for which I qualify. I understand that I am under no obligation to purchase any books, as explained on the opposite page. I am over 18 years of age.

BLOCK CAPITALS PLEASE

MS/MRS/MISS/MR _____

ADDRESS _____

_____

POSTCODE _____

 **WORTH FOUR FREE BOOKS**
PLUS A PUFFED HEART NECKLACE

 **WORTH FOUR FREE BOOKS**

 WORTH THREE FREE BOOKS

 WORTH TWO FREE BOOKS

DETACH AND POST CARD TODAY

The Reader Service™
FREEPOST
Croydon
Surrey
CR9 3WZ

NO
STAMP
NEEDED

several times whether that was the reason she'd been so wary around him.

Now that he knew that she was living with shadows too he was determined to take things slowly, to build up a friendship between them so that she would eventually learn to trust him enough to tell him about her pain.

His eyes focused on her soft pink lips and he remembered how they had responded to him, hotly and wildly, and he registered the swift reaction of his body with a silent groan.

He tightened his arm around her briefly, loath to let her go, but he had a feeling that it would be bad enough if Laura woke up to find that they'd slept together all night— no matter how innocently—without discovering that he was rampantly ready to destroy any semblance of that innocence.

CHAPTER SIX

'LAURA?'

The call was accompanied by a brisk tap on the door and Laura rolled over groggily.

'Come in,' she called, still more asleep than awake, as she glanced towards her alarm clock.

'Lazybones!' Hannah scolded cheerfully. 'You're usually up and ready by now. What happened? Did you forget to set your alarm? And why are you still dressed in yesterday's uniform?'

Laura glanced down at herself, and when she saw the way her bedspread was tucked around her crumpled form she suddenly remembered what had happened last night.

'I. . .er. . .must have fallen asleep beforc I had time to get ready for bed,' she mumbled as she dragged strangely shaky fingers through her tousled hair. She hoped fervently that the light in the room was too dim, and Hannah too busy with her barrage of questions, to notice that her face had just grown scarlet.

What *had* happened last night? All she could remember was curling up against Wolff in the close confines of the narrow bed. How long had he stayed? What had he thought when she. . .?

'Well, I hope you slept well,' Hannah continued brightly, 'because you've got just fifteen minutes before you're due on duty.'

'What? I'll never make it!'

98

Laura scrambled to her feet and looked wildly around the room, trying to decide what to do first.

'Oh, for goodness' sake!' Hannah said in exasperation. 'Have your shower and get dressed. I'll make you some coffee to see if we can jump-start your brain.'

'Thanks, Hannah. I don't know how I can have forgotten to set the alarm. . .'

She crossed her fingers superstitiously as she voiced the lie. She knew only too well how she'd come to forget to set her alarm. Once she'd been wrapped in Wolff's arms, with her head resting over the reassuring beat of his heart, the last thing she'd been thinking about was setting her alarm for work the next morning. She'd felt so comfortable and secure that for the first time in ages she'd slept as soundly as a baby.

So soundly, she thought exasperatedly as her mind went round in ever-decreasing circles, like the soapy water going down the drain, that she had no idea what time he had left her.

What must he have thought when she'd fallen asleep on him like that? She'd hardly been the most entertaining company. . .

'Here you are,' Hannah announced as she arrived with a steaming mug of coffee and a pile of hot buttered toast. 'Get some of that inside you.' She reached out and grabbed one slice for herself, and sat herself on the end of Laura's bed to watch her play the hairdryer over her wet hair.

'Thank you,' Laura mumbled around a crunchy mouthful. 'How am I doing for time?'

'OK so far. Keep going.' She retrieved Laura's shoes from under the end of her bed and nudged them towards her feet. 'It's not like you to be so disorganised,' she commented. 'You must have been very tired.'

'I certainly slept well,' Laura confirmed honestly. Well, it was true. She'd slept better in Wolff's arms that she had in. . .well, in years.

'Have you forgotten anything? Watch? Belt?' Hannah prompted.

'Brain?' Laura joked through the last mouthful of toast and chewed frantically, with the second half of her mug of coffee waiting to follow it down.

'All I can say is that it's a good thing that you're on half-day today,' Hannah teased. 'Perhaps your brain will catch up and you'll be firing on all cylinders by tomorrow!'

She continued to tease Laura all the way across to the A and E department, only allowing her to escape when Sister MacDonald wanted a word with her.

Laura had dumped her belongings in her locker and was on her way back to the reception area when Wolff appeared in the doorway of the kitchenette with a steaming mug in his hand.

Her eyes flicked over him in a lightning survey, noting with more than a spark of interest that while his clothes were different from those he'd worn yesterday his dark hair was nearly black with the remaining dampness from his own shower—and there was a tiny razor cut on the edge of his jaw, as if he'd had to shave in a hurry this morning.

'Good morning, sir,' she said, hoping that he couldn't hear the quiver of apprehension in her voice and that her face wasn't as hot as it felt.

So far, she hadn't had time to speak to anyone in the nurses' accommodation so no one had commented on the fact that she'd taken him up to her room last night, but she still wasn't confident that they hadn't been observed.

'Well, that answers one question,' he murmured in a husky voice, a teasing glint in his eyes. 'You called me "sir" so that must mean you still respect me the morning after.'

'Wolff!' she muttered with a nervous glance each way along the corridor. 'You start saying things like that and who knows how they'd be interpreted if people overheard?'

'I'm sorry,' he said, but his grin was unrepentant and so infectious that she couldn't help smiling back. 'Anyway, I'm glad I've seen you.'

'Oh?' Her heart skipped a beat and settled into a faster rhythm in spite of her silent battle for control.

He bent towards her, lending an air of intimacy to their conversation, and she was surrounded by the same mixture of fresh soap and indefinable musk which instantly reminded her of how it had felt to be wrapped securely in his arms.

'There were two things I wanted to talk about. . . First, I wanted to thank you,' he murmured, the silvery blue of his eyes skating over her face with a tender touch. 'I can't remember when I last slept so well.'

'You slept, too?' she demanded softly, helpless to stop the pleased smile spreading over her face. 'I thought I was the only one to drop off, and I've spent the last half-hour worrying about how rude I was.'

'It's all right. . .you didn't snore,' he teased, and she felt her cheeks heating again at the intimacy of the comment.

'What was the second thing?' she prompted, not quite certain how to cope with this new playful version of the tightly wound Wolff Bergen she'd thought she was getting to know. She hadn't taken part in this sort of repartee for years—shouldn't be indulging in it now—but there was something about him which she found absolutely irresistible.

'I wanted to ask you a favour,' he replied with an expression which was just too guileless to be true. 'I saw on the rota that you're on half-day today. . .' He paused, with one eyebrow raised in a question.

'Yes, but. . .'

'In that case, I wondered if you'd keep me company while I look at some flats this afternoon,' he said diffidently.

'Me? But. . .' Laura was quite startled by the unexpected request.

'I feel that I've burdened Leo long enough,' he explained. 'Especially as he hasn't been getting much sleep since I moved in with him.'

'By all accounts, he doesn't get a lot of sleep when you *aren't* there,' she replied with her tongue firmly in her cheek. 'Are you sure this isn't a male solidarity thing, and you just don't want to cramp his style any longer?'

'Either way, I've lined up some properties to look at and I'd like your input,' he said, swiftly sidestepping her comments about Leo's love life.

'But why me?' Laura asked in confusion. 'I don't know what sort of thing you're looking for.'

'Nor do I—in detail,' he admitted. 'But last night, when I saw how comfortable and individual you'd made your room in the nurses' accommodation, I thought that you would be a good person to spot the possibilities in a place.'

'Well. . .' She was aware that he was using his praise of the touches she'd added to her room in a deliberate

attempt to butter her up, but she was no more immune to
praise than the next person.

'I haven't really had time to make many friends yet,'
he continued softly. 'And Leo's on duty this afternoon,
and it's so *boring* looking at places without a friend along
to bounce ideas off. . .'

'All right! All right! Enough!' Laura begged with a
laugh. 'I'll go with you, if only to prevent you having to
invent another half a dozen reasons to make me agree.'

'Great!' he said with a smile. 'Where shall I meet you?'

'For heaven's sake!' she exclaimed in exasperation.
'We'll be working in the same department all morning.
It's hardly likely that we'll lose track of each other by
lunchtime! Now go and do some work!'

Laura sent him a mock glare and set off towards the
reception area once more, only just managing to turn the
corner before the urge to skip along the corridor was subdued under a broad smile.

She still wasn't quite certain why Wolff had gone to so
much trouble to persuade her to go with him this afternoon.
Did he have some nefarious scheme up his sleeve, such as
the exotic dance scheme of Leo's, or did he genuinely
think of her as a friend he could call upon to keep him
company while he did a boring chore?

Her thoughts were going round and round in her head
while she dealt with the usual mixture of ills and ailments
brought to the A and E department on a frosty November
morning.

Wolff was such an unlikely candidate for a friend, she
mused as she watched a young Lolita try to chat him up
while he was examining her for possible appendicitis.

From what the precocious youngster was saying, Laura

thought there was a good possibility that the painful epi-
sodes she was complaining about were the result of pelvic
inflammatory disease at best, or one of the more serious
sexually transmitted diseases at worst.

Laura hid a smile when she saw the way the back of
Wolff's neck reddened when his young patient volunteered
to spreadeagle herself for examination without a trace of
embarrassment.

She also heard genuine relief in his voice when he told
the forward young hussy that he was sending her up to the
obstetrics and gynaecology department where any necessary tests would be performed.

Laura would have loved to have teased him about his
endearing embarrassment, but there was no time. By the
sound of running feet their next patient was already on her
way into the emergency room, her terrified screams making
all the hair stand up on the back of Laura's neck.

'Please. . . Help my little girl. She's burnt. . .'

It was the mother who burst into the room first, wild-
eyed, with her child clutched in her arms.

'She fell over and her hand went on the fire. . .' reported
the ambulanceman who had followed immediately behind
her at a run, an IV bag held aloft and an Entonox cylinder
under one arm. 'She's been fighting the Entonox mask all
the way in. . .'

Almost before the words were out of his mouth Laura
was reaching out towards Wolff with a hypodermic needle
in one hand and a container of analgesic in the other, while
the ambulanceman finally managed to place the Entonox
mask over the child's nose and mouth.

The mother was standing just inside the door with her
little girl clutched in her arms, as if she was too scared to

let go of her, but it didn't make any difference to the speed of Wolff's reaction to the emergency.

The pain-relieving injection was administered almost before the child had realised what he was trying to do, and a second IV line was put in position and taped securely just in case they needed to increase her fluid intake in a hurry.

While Wolff was concerned with the chemical management of the child, trying to make certain that she didn't go into shock as a result of the trauma, Laura was giving the injured hand an extra-liberal coating of Water Jel and covering it with a fresh dressing.

'Can you bring her over to the table?' he asked the distraught mother over her child's pitiful cries, and he demonstrated how he wanted her to sit on the stool he usually used when he was in for a long stretch of stitching. She could then rest her daughter's weight on the supportive surface of the table while she could continue to reassure her with her encircling arms.

As the Entonox and analgesic began to work the poor scrap's blood-curdling shrieks slowly diminished into hiccuping sobs and whimpers.

The ambulanceman was finally able to make his full report, and when he left the room Laura saw him glance back sadly at his tiny passenger.

Wolff had examined the little hand as far as he could without disturbing the now-silent child too much, and he beckoned Laura across for a quick word.

'Will you monitor her while I speak to the burns unit?' he muttered. 'I've only had a quick look at the injury but I'm afraid that it's going to mean amputation so I want her looked at quickly.'

Laura nodded and watched as he spared a few seconds

to reassure the young mother and stroke the back of one finger over her child's tear-stained little cheek.

'She's only just learning to walk,' the young woman said when the doors swung closed behind Wolff. She looked up briefly from her pretty daughter, but was obviously desperate to talk. 'My boyfriend's mum bought her these new shoes and she wasn't used to them. . .'

Her throat closed up, preventing her from speaking for a moment, and Laura watched as she pressed her colourless lips tightly together in attempt to control her tears.

'I'd just taken the fireguard away to put some more coal on when she tripped over the edge of the rug in front of the fireplace and fell towards the flames. She put her hand out to try to save herself. . .I couldn't catch her in time to save her. . .'

She shook her head, unable to continue for the force of her silent sobs.

'Dr Bergen has gone to see how quickly they can get a bed ready for her in the children's burns unit,' Laura told her, knowing that she would want to know what was going on. 'As soon as he gets back he'll tell you what's happening.'

There was no reason to tell her that he'd left the room to make his call because he also wanted to tell the consultant how serious the injuries were—there was plenty of time for the poor woman to find that out.

'Will I be able to go up with her? She's never been away from me before.'

'Of course you can,' Laura reassured her as she checked the child's vital signs again, smiling at the solemn expression in her watchful hazel eyes. At least the analgesic meant that she wasn't in pain any more. . .

'They've even got a limited number of beds available so that you can stay overnight,' she added, remembering the special arrangements the hospital made for parents of their younger patients.

'Oh, thank you.' She drew in a shuddering breath, a little colour stealing its way back into her face.

'I don't know how I'm going to tell my boyfriend what's happened. He's working shifts, and if I'm not there when he gets home he's going to worry where we are.'

'Have you got a neighbour you can call?' Laura asked. 'Perhaps they'd be willing to give him a message for you?'

Ideally, Laura would have liked to be able to contact the young woman's boyfriend so that he could come straight to the hospital. She had a feeling that the mother was going to need all the support she could get if the injury was as serious as Wolff thought.

'The lady over the road might. . .' she was musing aloud as Wolff returned.

'It's all organised,' he announced with a reassuring smile on his face. 'There's a bed on the unit and it will be ready and waiting by the time the two of you get up there.'

As he spoke a porter came through the door, pushing a wheelchair, and in no time they had her sitting in the chair with her daughter cradled safely in her arms.

Wolff gave a final check of the child's vital signs, filled in his findings on her chart and then draped the IV bags over the porter's shoulder ready for the journey.

'Good luck,' Laura murmured with a consoling squeeze of the woman's slender shoulder as she was wheeled away. 'They'll do everything they can for her.'

'How bad do you think it is?'

Laura couldn't help asking, wondering just what sort of

handicap the little scrap was going to have to grow up with.

'It looks as if she gripped the hot bar at the top of the fender in front of the hearth when she fell because at least two fingers received full-thickness burns. They'll probably have to take both of them away because they're too badly injured to survive and they daren't risk gangrene.'

'And the rest of the hand?' Laura asked, feeling slightly sick.

'She'll have scarring on the other fingers where they were seared by the heat but, with any luck, they'll still be viable.' His expression was grim. 'I suppose the only good thing we can say about it is that at least she didn't land on her face.'

Laura shuddered at the thought.

'Her poor mother is never going to be able to forgive herself,' she murmured as she completed the tidying-up routine. 'Every time she sees her daughter's little hand she's going to blame herself for not catching her in time.'

Wolff murmured his agreement and sighed.

'I'm ready for a break,' he said, and when Laura looked up at the clock on the wall she realised that she was due a few minutes off too.

'Whose turn is it to put the kettle on?' she asked, still subdued by the sadness of their last case.

'Mine, I think,' he said as he pushed the door open for her and they stepped out into the corridor.

'Doctor?' Celia MacDonald's familiar Scots accent floated along the corridor towards them. 'Could you come here a minute, please?'

Wolff grimaced and shrugged wryly.

'Obviously there's no peace for the wicked,' he grumbled as he set off after the senior sister.

'Do you want me to come, too?' Laura offered. The thought of a cup of coffee wasn't nearly as enticing if she wasn't going to be sharing Wolff's company at the same time.

'Please,' Wolff said with a smile, and Laura's heart grew just a little bit lighter.

'This is Sharron Ferguson,' Big Mac announced when they joined her in the far treatment room. 'She's fourteen years old and weighs twenty-two stones. This. . .' she indicated an even more gargantuan figure overflowing a chair beside the trolley '. . .is her mother.'

The introductions were interrupted by a rising moan from the daughter who writhed awkwardly, rather like a beached whale.

While Wolff read the notes Laura busied herself by gathering an examining tray and a fresh set of gloves until Sister MacDonald could make herself heard again.

'As you can see, she's suffering intermittent abdominal pain of rising severity. She's menstruating at the moment and she's never been sexually active.'

When she heard the last two details Laura's first guess— that the obese youngster was in labour—had to be replaced with several other possibilities.

Perhaps she had eaten something to which she had an allergy, or was very constipated or had some other form of bowel obstruction. Or it might be that her appendix was either about to rupture or had already done so, and she was starting to suffer the symptoms of peritonitis.

She listened while Wolff questioned the girl, watching him grow steadily more frustrated when her mother answered every question and gave him little or no useful information.

He'd waited until she was between bouts of pain before he tried to palpate the tender region of her stomach, but Laura could tell from the expression on his face that the girl was so grossly overweight that he couldn't determine anything helpful.

'So, Sharron,' he recapped after several minutes, 'you've been in pain intermittently for about twelve hours and you've been sick a couple of times. You've never been pregnant. . .'

'How could she have been pregnant when no one's ever touched her. . .down there?' interrupted her mother belligerently. 'I've told you. She only started her monthlies two years ago and they're not regular yet.'

'And you haven't noticed any particular weight loss or weight gain recently?' Wolff persevered.

'She's put on about six stone in the last year or so,' her mother confirmed wearily as her daughter's wails grew louder again. 'Look, when are you going to do something to help her? She's in pain.'

'Before we can do anything to help we have to know what's the matter,' Wolff said patiently. 'And to do that I'm going to have to take a blood sample and then examine your daughter so if you'd like to help her take her clothes off and put a gown on. . .'

'How many of her clothes?' demanded her mother suspiciously. 'I've heard about you doctors interfering with women. . .down there.'

'That's why the nurse will be with us the whole time,' he replied with admirable calm. 'To make sure that I can't do anything I shouldn't, and that I can't be accused of something I didn't do.'

'Well, that's as maybe but you still aren't touching her...down there,' she said stoutly.

In spite of Wolff's patient explanations, it seemed as if they had reached stalemate—until Sharron's pain seemed to grow suddenly worse.

For the first time it looked as if her mother was wavering in her conviction, and Laura pressed home the message.

'When the pain is that bad it could be a sign that there's something seriously wrong,' she said earnestly. 'The examination will only take a couple of minutes, and if we can find out what's causing the pain then we'll know what to do to stop it.'

Sharron began to writhe again, shouting out like a soul in torment, and her mother finally caved in.

Moving swiftly in case she changed her mind, Laura draped a sheet over the heavily sweating youngster and helped her out of her blood-stained underwear before Wolff sat himself on a stool at the foot of the trolley with a speculum in his hand.

He hadn't even had time to position the instrument when there was a sudden gush of blood-streaked fluid all down his disposable apron.

A wet shiny object covered in thick black hair appeared between his patient's legs, and it was so swiftly expelled that he only just managed to catch it as it fell towards the floor.

Laura gasped and Wolff looked up from his contemplation of the wriggling mass in his hands with a shocked expression.

Training kicked in then and, although they didn't usually end up delivering babies in the emergency department, Laura was quick to grab the right sterile pack so that Wolff could clamp and cut the cord and then suction the tiny nose and mouth.

'Here you are,' he murmured, seeming almost shell-shocked by the speed of events as he stood up and laid the baby boy on the new mother's stomach.

'That's not mine!' shrieked the youngster, looking at the blood-smeared infant in horror as he started to utter the familiar newborn's cry.

'That's not hers!' echoed her mother, glaring balefully at each of them in turn.

'Well, it's certainly not mine,' said Wolff with a masterful attempt at keeping a straight face. 'So, if you'll forgive me for a minute, I'll just let the maternity ward know that they've got another customer waiting for collection.'

It was another half-hour before Laura finally managed to sit down for a drink.

In the meantime, it seemed as if everyone in A and E had heard about Wolff's 'special delivery'.

'The local football team could do with him in goal,' joked one of the porters, the first person to stop her and ask for confirmation of the story.

'Does *everyone* know?' she asked Hannah after the twentieth comment.

'Well, it was a bit difficult to miss it,' Hannah pointed out with a grin. 'You must admit there was an awful lot of shouting going on in there.'

'It did get a bit noisy,' Laura agreed wryly as she remembered the combined volume of the belligerent mother and her beached whale of a daughter.

It still amazed her that the fourteen-year-old could still

deny having ever been touched by a man while she was in the throes of advanced labour.

But the saddest part, as far as Laura was concerned, was the fact that the first thing that gorgeous healthy little boy had known was instant rejection.

If he had been hers. . .

She squeezed her eyes tight shut, concentrating on controlling the temptation to cry at the unfairness of life.

The sadness hung over her for the rest of the morning, casting a shadow over her proposed outing with Wolff.

In all probability, once the nurses and midwives took Sharron and her baby son in hand she would realise that, although he was unexpected, there was no reason why the precious gift she'd been given should be unwanted or unloved.

The situation was still playing on her mind as she waited for Wolff to meet her at the end of her shift.

'Sorry to keep you waiting in the cold,' he panted after a swift sprint across the car park. 'Can you grab these while I unlock?' He thrust a sheaf of papers at her and rummaged through his pockets for his keys.

Laura gazed down at the bundle of estate agent's details he'd handed her, but out of the corner of her eye she was cataloguing the way his washed-to-death jeans fitted the lean perfection of his body. If there was anything which could take her mind off her own troubles it was this man. . .

'I did a quick detour after I handed over,' Wolff said as he settled himself behind the wheel of the car. He'd impressed Laura with his old-fashioned courtesy when he'd made a point of opening the passenger door first to let her get in out of the cold.

It had also given her a chance for some more surreptitious ogling as she watched his long fluid strides take him round the front of the car to his own door.

She liked the way he looked in his comfortably worn casual clothes. It seemed as if most of the nurses had commented on how different he looked after he'd been forced to change out of his suit trousers and leather shoes when baby Ferguson had liberally coated them with amniotic fluid.

She managed to subdue the smile which threatened and concentrated on his words.

'If something more urgent has come up I don't mind if you want to put this outing off,' she offered.

'No way!' he objected. 'I've been looking forward to this all morning. It was the only thing which made all the teasing after that unexpected delivery bearable!'

'You've been fending off enquiries and jokes, too?' she said and they both laughed.

'There's a map with those papers I handed you,' he said, pausing to concentrate on his driving as he turned out of the hospital grounds and onto the main road. 'Could you direct us to the first place I've marked—a red dot?'

Laura found the mark and gave him directions for their first port of call.

'Actually, that's where I went just now,' he said as he indicated for the first of several turns. 'I went to find out how "our" baby was doing.'

'How is he?' Laura demanded eagerly, all thought of navigating gone. She could have kicked herself for not thinking of doing the same thing. It would have stopped her worrying about. . .

'It doesn't look very hopeful,' Wolff said with a scowl as he indicated again and pulled up outside a very dilapidated-looking house, crudely divided into flats.

'What doesn't?' she enquired, muddled by the effort of sorting out two separate conversations. 'The flat?'

'Oh, *that* won't do at all,' he agreed as he pulled back out into the flow of traffic and asked for the next set of directions. 'But I was talking about the baby.'

'Why?' Laura demanded, worry jolting through her like a fierce blow. 'What's wrong with him? He seemed fine when he left us—his Apgar was almost perfect.'

'Oh, there's nothing wrong with *him*,' he said, rapidly putting her mind at rest on that score. '*He's* doing fine. It's his mother and grandmother who are the problem.'

'Why?' she repeated with a feeling of dread, her eyes deserting the map entirely to focus on the steely expression on Wolff's face.

'They've completely rejected the little chap,' he said angrily. 'They say they don't want him. . .that he's going to be put up for adoption.'

CHAPTER SEVEN

LAURA could hear from Wolff's voice that he was disgusted, but she was utterly devastated by the news.

How could people *think* about abandoning their own flesh and blood? She realised that Sharron was too young, but it wasn't as if she wouldn't have her own mother's help. How could they bear to just give her baby away? Didn't they want to watch him grow and develop...to watch the changes as he became a toddler, a schoolchild, a teenager and finally a man?

She was aware that her inner debate was making her a less than ideal companion, but she couldn't seem to switch it off.

Several times she caught Wolff's thoughtful gaze on her, his blue eyes seeming to try to work out what was troubling her. He was obviously making allowances for her strange mood, keeping up a flow of easy chatter as they criss-crossed the town looking at everything from detached gothic horrors to tiny modern flats whose fixtures and fittings were the epitome of yuppie self-indulgence.

If she'd had to pick her favourite Laura would have had to admit that the last one they visited had held her attention the longest. Its decorative mixture of soft neutrals and earth colours with honey-coloured wood seemed to welcome her with warmth as soon as they stepped inside, in spite of the fact that it was empty and the heating was turned off.

'What do you think?' Wolff said as he surveyed the

spacious-looking lounge again at the end of their tour. 'This one looks as if it's ready to move straight into.'

'It's very nice,' Laura agreed with a distracted half-smile. She was staring blindly at the fading daylight outside the bay window, the pain which she usually managed to keep hidden inside the darkest corner of her heart creeping out like some sort of virulent cancer to cast a pall over everything.

'Laura?'

The change in tone of Wolff's voice drew her attention back to him.

'What's the matter?' he questioned kindly. 'Aren't you feeling very well. . .or have I bored you into insensibility?'

'Oh, Wolff, I'm sorry,' she said, stricken to realise that she'd hardly done more than answer in monosyllables all afternoon. 'I've been an utter wet blanket, haven't I?'

'Is it. . .?' He hesitated. 'I don't like to sound like a male chauvinist pig, but it seemed to come on so suddenly. Is it what Mrs Ferguson would call your monthlies?'

Laura gazed at him in dismay, too shocked to feel any embarrassment at the topic of the conversation.

Of all the things he could have said, what on earth had put *that* into his head?

Suddenly the implications of the whole day overcame her and she burst into tears.

'Oh, God! Laura, I'm sorry,' Wolff muttered as he hovered beside her for one brief second as if he had no idea what to do with a weeping woman.

Then he acted, wrapping both arms around her and drawing her as tightly as he could against the warmth and security of his broad chest.

'I'm sorry,' Laura wailed, mortified that she'd lost control over such a stupid thing. In two years she had never broken down like this. 'Oh, Wolff, I feel such a fool.'

'Shh, Laura, shh!' he soothed as he cupped his hand around the back of her head and cradled it against him, rocking her as though she were a frightened child.

Eventually he produced a large handkerchief and proceeded to mop her face dry before he handed it to her to blow her nose and stepped away.

'Better?' he enquired, and when she nodded she saw him glance down at the slim watch strapped to his wrist.

'Have you got another appointment?' she asked, drawing in a shaky breath as she straightened her shoulders and prepared to leave.

'No. I was just checking to see if the estate agent's office was still open. I'd like to put my name down for this one before anyone else has a chance to.'

Laura was almost breathless with the speed of his decision, and totally distracted from her own concerns.

'Are you certain you don't want to see any others?' she cautioned. 'You've only been looking for a couple of hours.'

'I went through a small forest of details to draw up a short list of the ones which met my five most important criteria—they had to be the right size, within my price-range, empty. . .so that I can move straight in and within reasonable travelling distance of the hospital in case I get called in to an emergency.'

'And?' she prompted. 'You said *five* criteria—size, price, ready to move in straight away, distance and. . .?'

'And *you* have to give your seal of approval,' he said with an outrageous grin. 'So, as this one fulfilled all five, it must be the one.'

Laura wouldn't have thought that she would find herself laughing so soon, but Wolff seemed to be developing the knack for lifting her out of herself with nothing more than a bit of nonsense.

'Let's lock up and get back to the car,' he suggested, suddenly seeming to be in a hurry. 'I've got the mobile phone in there to get hold of the estate agent, and we can drop the keys off on the way back.'

Laura followed in his wake, casting one last look over her shoulder at the welcoming atmosphere in the little house before she resigned herself to the end of her outing with Wolff.

She sat beside him in the car while he made the estate agent's day with a speedy sale, but her thoughts were in a hopeless muddle.

In spite of her preoccupation, she'd enjoyed spending time with him. He'd been such good company that she wasn't looking forward to returning to her room, knowing that she would end up shut inside the four walls with the memories that, today, were haunting her more than ever.

It didn't take long for Wolff to leap out of the car and lean in through the office door to hand the bunch of keys to the agent, not even bothering to walk all the way inside the office.

Laura heard him promise to come back as soon as they let him know everything was ready for signing, and then he was climbing back into the car.

'When he hears that I found what I was looking for Leo's going to be a very happy man,' he commented wryly as he started the engine.

'I thought you were staying with him because the two of you were friends?'

'We have been for, oh, it must be ten years at least,' he agreed. 'But, as the saying goes, guests and fish stink after three days, and I've already been with him for four.'

Laura was still laughing at the wry accuracy of the quip when she suddenly realised that they were going the wrong way.

'Wolff, you should have turned the other way back there. The nurses' accommodation is the other side of the hospital.'

'Actually, I was hoping you'd help me to celebrate my new status as a nearly-householder,' he said casually. 'As you helped me to choose, the least I can do is offer you a cup of coffee or a glass of wine—if Leo hasn't found the bottle I hid in the back of the fridge.'

Laura was so pleased that their afternoon together wasn't over yet that she nearly missed the searching look he threw her way.

Suddenly she remembered just how sharp this man's mind was, and realised that his offer of hospitality was probably nothing more than an excuse to pin her down with questions until she told him why she'd broken down this afternoon.

Even though a shiver of apprehension raised goose bumps up her arms she still couldn't regret the chance to spend more time with him.

For all that he gave the appearance of being a typical footloose bachelor and far too handsome for his own good, she had discovered over the last few days that there was another Wolff carefully hidden under that façade—a Wolff who made her feel good about herself made her feel feminine and womanly for the first time in two years. . .for all the good it would do her.

It was that last thought which accompanied her as Wolff let them into Leo's little flat, but the sight which met her eyes as he shut the door behind them drove everything else out of her mind.

'Oh-h-h,' she breathed in horror when she saw the state of the room.

'Exactly,' Wolff muttered, sounding almost embarrassed about the chaos that confronted them. 'Leo's actually quite a tidy person, but you'd never know it from this mess. A flat this small was never designed to cram two sets of possessions into.'

'You're right there,' Laura agreed as she wondered where on earth they were going to sit to have the drink Wolff had offered her.

'Perhaps you can understand now why I was so keen to find a place of my own as soon as possible,' he said as he picked up an armful of belongings from the small settee, then looked around helplessly for somewhere else to put them.

'Here. . .' Laura amalgamated two piles on the sturdy coffee-table. 'Will that fit there?'

'Thanks,' he growled sheepishly as he deposited his burden. 'At least that clears a place to sit. Sometimes I wonder if it's actually breeding and we'll get buried under it one night and never be seen again!'

Laura chuckled at the thought as he went to get their drinks.

As she shrugged out of her parka she realised that there was nowhere obvious to hang it so she lay it over the high back of the settee, then settled herself onto its surprisingly comfortable cushions.

'Here you are,' Wolff said, holding out a glass of pale

straw-coloured liquid, the tiny bubbles rising through it like miniature strings of beads.

'Leo didn't find it, then,' she commented, suddenly nervous now that he'd come back into the room. She could see that there was only one place for him to sit, but she didn't know how she would cope with having him sitting so close.

It was one thing to innocently fall asleep beside him when tiredness overtook her, or to accept the comfort of his strong arms when she was upset, but the only other time she had been this close to Wolff Bergen had been the very first time they'd met when he'd danced with her as intimately as if they'd been long-time lovers.

'Relax,' he whispered and leant back into his corner, proving once again that he had an uncanny ability to discern her thoughts. It was a strange feeling, and the proximity of his long legs to hers didn't make it any easier.

She glanced up at him, his tanned face seeming even darker in the subdued lighting and his eyes strangely lighter as though lit from within with a soft radiance.

She took a sip from her wine and tried to calm her nervousness by thinking about the shift she'd just finished.

Suddenly she had a mental image of the second when Sharron and her jet-propelled baby had showered his smart clothes with unexpected fluids, and she couldn't help the grin which crept over her face.

'What?' he demanded, although she hadn't said a word.

'Nothing, really. I was just wondering whether your shoes will ever recover,' she said with a chuckle. 'And I'd love to be a fly on the wall when you take those trousers into the dry-cleaners and explain what sort of stain removal they're going to need.'

'Sometimes I think you've got a very twisted sense of humour,' Wolff complained in a pained voice, but then he met her eyes and they were both laughing.

Laura sipped again and slowly she lost her smile.

'He was a beautiful baby, wasn't he?' she commented as her mental replay of the morning's events rolled on and her throat grew tight.

'Beautiful?' Wolff questioned in a voice full of amazement. 'He looked like a very bald, very wrinkled, very angry old man. You women are all the same. You grow positively misty-eyed over every one of them, no matter what they look like.'

Laura knew he was teasing and tried to give him an answering smile, but her lips were trembling too much.

'Dammit, I've done it again,' she heard him mutter when he saw the tears glittering in her eyes.

He reached for the wine glass, which was perilously close to losing its contents, and deposited it under the coffee-table with his own, then he slid one arm behind her shoulders and pulled her close.

'Ah, Laura, tell me what's the matter,' he demanded softly. 'I can't bear it when you look so hurt and desperate, and I seem to be causing it. . .'

'No.' She shook her head and drew in a steadying breath. 'It's not you, Wolff. It's. . . It's. . .' How did she begin? *Where* did she begin?

'Shall I tell you how far I've got in working things out, and then you can tell me where I've gone wrong?'

He didn't wait for her agreement and she was grateful that she didn't have to try to make a decision.

'It doesn't take a genius to work out that it's got something to do with babies,' he began matter-of-factly. 'You

were a little subdued after the baby was born this morning
but you were perfectly all right earlier this afternoon—
right up until I told you the Fergusons wanted to give their
baby away.'

Laura was almost frozen with shock. She'd had two
years of practice at hiding her thoughts and feelings and
had no idea that she was still so easy to read.

'Now we come to the part I haven't worked out,' Wolff
continued. 'As far as I can tell, you're about twenty-five
years old. . .'

'Twenty-six,' Laura corrected, and he inclined his head
in acceptance.

'Close enough for my purposes,' he conceded
graciously. 'And, although I can't understand why someone
as gorgeous as you hasn't been snapped up long ago and
chained to a kitchen sink, twenty-six is far too young for
you to be feeling as if you've been left on the shelf so it's
unlikely that babies are setting off the alarm button on
your biological clock. . .'

He let his voice die away in an obvious invitation for
her to supply the *real* reason.

'Sorry. No prizes,' Laura said with a bitterness she
couldn't hide. 'For some of us the biological clock starts
ticking at a much faster rate than the rest, and we can run
out of time before we even realise that there's a deadline.'

'What?' His forehead pleated in thought as he tried to
decipher the meaning of her words. 'Do you mean that
you've had an accident, or surgery, and it's affected your
reproductive system?'

'You're getting closer,' she said lightly, trying to make
a joke out of the situation before she embarrassed herself

again. 'Only in my case it's endometriosis which has stopped my clock.'

'Stopped it?' he queried instantly. 'I know there are a small number of women who suffer from it early, but you're very young for it to be that advanced.'

'As far as my fiancé was concerned, it might just as well have done,' she said as the anger and despair welled up inside her. 'I'd been having some problems—ever since the onset of puberty, in fact—and when he proposed I decided to get things checked out.'

She stared blindly at the calendar hanging lopsidedly on the wall, not even registering what the picture was about as she remembered.

'We'd talked about when we wanted to start a family and how many children we wanted. . .' She drew in a shuddering breath and continued doggedly.

'The results of the tests came through the day we were going to celebrate our engagement, and when I told him I was so upset that it might disrupt all our lovely plans that he suggested putting off the party. I didn't realise that he meant to put it off permanently until he announced his engagement to one of my colleagues three months later.'

'Bastard,' Wolff hissed venomously as he tightened his arm protectively around her.

'He's not really,' she admitted, her voice seeming to echo in the emptiness inside her. 'He's a paediatrician and he's always loved children.'

'But if he were any sort of a man he'd be marrying a woman because he loved her, not because she was going to be his brood mare,' Wolff pointed out fiercely.

Laura had to smile at the way he'd instantly leapt to her defence and she rested her head gratefully on his shoulder.

They sat in silence for a moment, but she could almost hear the thoughts whirling round in Wolff's brain before he spoke again.

'Did your results say you'd never be able to have children?' he asked, obviously pursuing the loose ends of her story.

'The specialist said that my chances would decrease rapidly as time went on. He seemed to think that if I hadn't had any children by the time I reached thirty then it was unlikely I would ever conceive.'

She was proud of the steady way she had delivered his verdict, even though it felt just as though her heart were being cut out with a blunt knife.

'Did you ever consider artificial insemination?' Wolff asked.

His voice was as calm as if he were commenting on the weather, but it released a tornado of unexpected thoughts inside her head.

'I considered it,' she said with a lift of her chin. 'Like St Augustine's, my last hospital had a fertility clinic, but in the end there were too many factors against it.'

'Such as?' he challenged.

'Such as. . .the fact that I'm single and they understandably prefer to concentrate their limited resources on couples. Such as the likelihood of success in the limited time I would have available to try. Such as the fact that, although patients' records are supposed to have a degree of confidentiality, there's little chance of preserving your privacy when the hospital grapevine will pick up on the fact that you're seen going into the fertility clinic on a regular basis.'

'You don't mean you'd be put off by the possibility of embarrassment?'

'Not so much for myself but for the child,' she pointed out. 'Can you imagine what it would be like to have all your mother's colleagues and friends knowing all the private details of your conception?'

He conceded the point with a nod but it was absent-minded, as if his restless brain had whirled on to consider other things.

'I take it from your reaction to events today,' he began slowly and thoughtfully, as if he was working out something complicated as he spoke. 'I take it that you'd still like a family of your own?'

'Oh, Wolff,' she breathed as the longing welled up inside her again and she looked up into his fiercely intent gaze. 'If only you knew how much. . .'

There was a long moment of silence as he absorbed the fervency of her words.

'I've had an idea. . .' he murmured softly, and Laura could have screamed with frustration when he didn't continue.

'What?' she questioned eagerly with a sudden hopeful leap of her heart. 'What idea?'

He was silent for so long that she began to wonder if she'd imagined those hopeful words.

'No,' he said at last.

The word was so final that it was like a slap in the face and she gasped at the impact.

'Ah, Laura, I'm sorry,' he said when he saw the stricken expression which she knew must be filling her eyes. 'I didn't mean that the idea was no good, just that it's too

soon to say any more. I need to do a bit of research before
I tell you what I'm thinking of.'

'But. . .'

'I'd love to tell you,' he said, a strange electric excitement seeming to sizzle through him as he gazed deep into
her eyes, 'but I don't want to get your hopes up until I've
checked some details. Please. . .' he continued when she
would have begged him to explain. 'Trust me?' he
whispered.

Laura subsided, defeated.

She might have known him for only a few days but she
did trust him, and if he said he needed to do some research
before he presented her with his idea then she was just
going to have to wait.

'How long?' she demanded impatiently, and he
chuckled, the sound deep and rich in the cluttered room.

'I hope, for both our sakes, that I'll have found out what
I need to know in a couple of days.'

'A couple of days!' she remonstrated and he
laughed again.

'You sound like a child waiting for Christmas to come,'
he said, and suddenly they both grew serious at the impli-
cation of his words.

A child. . .

'Oh, Wolff,' she whispered, her heart full to overflowing
that he was interested enough to try to find a way round
her problem. It was more than Peter had ever done, and
he was supposed to have loved her enough to marry her. . .

'Thank you,' she said fervently. 'Even if it doesn't come
to anything, thank you for trying. Thank you for being
there and for listening. . .'

She reached up and cradled his cheek, loving the sandpapery roughness of his chin against her palm as she tilted his face towards her own and pressed her lips to his.

The sensation was electric, every nerve in her body responding to the warmth and the subtle sliding of his mouth as he took over control.

They'd kissed before, but the circumstances of that first time had been so outlandish that she hadn't believed that her memories could be accurate.

In the end she'd dismissed them as fantasies, produced by terror, embarrassment and too much wine.

Blood didn't boil like it did in her memory and nerves didn't sizzle. . .

Except that it was happening again, and this time neither of them had done more than sip a glass of wine.

She was vaguely aware that she was probably going to feel very embarrassed afterwards when she remembered how avidly she was wrapping herself around his body, her fingers revelling in the silky density of his thick dark hair and the warm strength of his neck and shoulders.

But for the moment the only fear she was feeling was that he might stop kissing her.

Wolff groaned when he finally tore his mouth away and rested his forehead against hers, and Laura echoed the sound, missing the soft stroke of his tongue across the tender inner surfaces of her lips and the possessive way he'd duelled with her own inside the warm darkness.

'Ah, Laura, if we didn't need to breathe. . .' he muttered, his voice huskier than ever, and with a wild leap of her heart Laura realised that he had been every bit as affected by their kiss as she had. 'And if Leo's car hadn't just pulled up outside. . .'

It took several seconds for the words to register, but

when they did Laura all but leapt out of his arms, frantically dragging her fingers through the short feathery strands of her hair to try to bring them back into some semblance of order. At least her clothing was still neat, even though she'd desperately wanted the constricting layers to disappear without trace not two minutes ago.

'Don't worry about it,' Wolff advised lazily as he sprawled back in his corner of the settee like a well-fed cat.

A wicked grin curled the corners of his mouth when he saw how flustered she was, but it wasn't until she saw the gleam in his eyes as they travelled over her that she realised that he was still consumed by desire, too.

'You look beautiful,' he murmured, his voice a husky purr which defied her to regain any sort of normal rhythm to either her heartbeat or her breathing. It sounded the way she imagined it would if they were in bed together, with even less between them than when she'd wrapped her arms around his naked shoulders on the stage.

She tried to block the mental image of what he would look like without the exotic waistcoat hiding the width of his chest, tried vainly to prevent herself from imagining what it would feel like to strip the rest of their clothes away until the two of them were naked and then. . .

'Laura,' he growled, a clear warning in his voice, 'if you don't stop looking at me like that there will be three very embarrassed people here when Leo walks in that door.'

Laura felt the heat rise in her cheeks and she couldn't look at him—*daren't* look at him—because, for the first time in years, she was enjoying the fact that her body was vibrantly aroused and Wolff seemed to be able to read her very thoughts.

'You're not the only one,' he muttered wryly as he shifted his position on the settee and leant forward to plant his elbows on his thighs. 'Leo would only have to take one look at me and he'd know what *I've* been thinking about.'

Laura couldn't help her sly smile of pleasure that *his* body's reaction was lingering, too. She'd been fully aware of his reaction to her the first time they'd kissed—it had been unavoidable, the way their bodies had been plastered together from breast to ankle—but their cramped position on the settee right now meant that she hadn't been nearly close enough to tell if their kiss had affected him the same way.

'Hi, Wolff,' Leo said tiredly as he swung the door closed with an elbow. He used the same elbow to hit the main light switch, then realised as brightness flooded the room that they had company.

'Oh, hello, Laura,' he added with less than his usual enthusiasm. 'Just to warn you for when you go in to work—it looks as if there's a bad batch of drugs on the street. We've had two doses so far, both fatal.'

He leant dejectedly back against the door with an armful of belongings, a carrier bag full of familiar foil containers and a miserable expression on his face.

'Leo, old friend,' Wolff greeted him with cheerfully smiling *bonhomie*. 'Before you sink into terminal depression at the trauma of coming home to this horrible sight at the end of a tough shift I've got some good news for you... I've found my own place.'

'Really?' Leo's strange golden eyes brightened instantly with guilty relief. 'That was quick. Where is it and when do you move?'

'It's a small house in a road on the other side of the

hospital from here, and it's in good enough decorative order for me to move in as soon as the legalities are taken care of. Laura helped me find it this afternoon.'

'Did she, now?' Leo said with a knowing tone in his newly vitalised voice and a roguish smile. 'In which case, Laura, I will be eternally in your debt. Ask anything you want and it shall be yours—my clothes, my body, my firstborn child—anything but my *moo goo gai pan* because I'm starving!'

They laughed when he tried to wrap his heavily laden arm protectively around the containers in the carrier bag and Laura noticed that his step was very much lighter as he went to get himself a plate.

He returned to the cluttered room in seconds, with his other belongings still clutched under one elbow.

'Can I help you with those?' Laura offered, jumping to her feet to relieve him of his ungainly burden. 'Where shall I put your jacket? Can I hang it up?'

'Thanks. If you could put it on the hook on the back of the door. . .' He pointed with an elbow.

There was the familiar shape of a hanger sticking out from under another jacket and Laura reached for it, intending to hang Leo's jacket up properly.

The only problem was that the hanger wasn't empty.

'Oh!' Laura exclaimed as she drew out a familiar waist-coat, the overhead light gleaming on the metallic threads the same way the spotlight had on the night she'd first met Wolff.

'Oh, no,' she heard his familiar husky voice mutter as she turned to face him, an impish smile curving her mouth as she held the hanger up.

'Yours, I believe?' she questioned wickedly. 'I seem

to recognise the waistcoat and the bow tie. . .but I don't remember seeing *this* part of the costume last time. . .'

She hooked one finger through the elastic and held up the skimpy matching G-string underwear, swinging it gently to and fro for a minute before she added thoughtfully, 'You know, if you'd worn *that* on the night you wouldn't have had to worry about *anyone* recognising you—they wouldn't have been looking at your face at all!'

CHAPTER EIGHT

LAURA was still chuckling when she went to bed that night.

The expression on Wolff's face had been priceless, especially the deep colour which had flooded his cheeks.

With the typical disloyalty of a friend of long standing, Leo had joined in with the story of Wolff's refusal to stand in for the professional dancer unless he was allowed to modify the costume.

'He was supposed to strip off to reveal that gorgeous little number before he danced with the winner but chickened out,' Leo had accused with a return to his usual wicked sense of humour. 'And it's not as if he's got anything to be ashamed of either. He's actually in quite good shape for an old man.'

'Old man?' Wolff had yelped. 'You're only two months younger than I am so watch who you're calling old.'

Wolff had straightened up out of the settee with his usual swift, economic grace and stepped aside to allow Leo access to the only available seat in the room.

'Here, sit down and rest,' he'd offered with a gleam in his eye which promised retaliation. 'You'd better save your strength for eating—while you've still got enough teeth. It's amazing how age can creep up on you.'

He'd suggested driving Laura back to her room then and, while she'd been loath to miss watching the easy way Wolff and Leo teased and insulted each other, she'd been glad to be leaving. So much had happened today that she'd needed some quiet time to absorb it all—not least the possibility that Wolff might have found a way for her to achieve her dearest wish.

Unfortunately, whatever lucky chance had been making certain that their shifts coincided had obviously deserted them now, and she'd been working with several other members of the A and E staff while they coped with another fatality and three near-misses as the bad batch of heroin took its toll on the drug-taking fraternity.

When Leo had told Wolff about the first two accidental doses Wolff had confirmed the newly familiar maxim in emergency care that if you had one get ready for several— and he'd been right.

Laura's memories and thoughts of Wolff were all she had to sustain her because for three days she hadn't seen him at all. Nor had he made any attempt to contact her outside the hospital.

Slowly the bright daydreams she had started to build about the fulfilment of her longing to be a mother started to fade, and the lightness in her step and the sparkle in her eyes dwindled into dull normality.

Even the prospect of a whole day off wasn't enough to cheer her up at the end of a long tiring shift.

She gazed out at the surrounding darkness as she zipped her parka up to her chin and braced herself to brave the bone-chilling rain.

The light streaming out across the car park showed her that the torrential downpour was being blown along almost horizontally by an unforgiving wind, and she shuddered in anticipation of the soaking she was going to get.

If only she'd listened to the weather report this morning

she'd have driven her car the few hundred yards around to this side of the hospital. Even if it had cost her money for petrol at least she wouldn't be getting soaked.

'Laura?'

Only half a dozen steps into her miserable journey her hair was already soaked and her ears were being buffeted unmercifully, but she could have sworn that she'd heard Wolff's husky voice calling her name.

'Hey, Laura! Over here!'

When the call was repeated she caught sight of a car in the no-parking zone to one side of the main entrance, an arm waving at her from the open window and a plume of white at the exhaust telling her that the engine was running.

Her heart leapt inside her chest when Wolff leant out of the open window to wave again, and she recognised the familiar shape of his head.

Laura hesitated for just a second, terrified by the implications of her joy at seeing him, but then she found that her feet were taking her towards him without conscious thought—unable to resist her strong desire to get closer to him.

It didn't seem to matter that he seemed to have ignored her for three days—she was still delighted to see him.

She'd only met him for the first time a week ago, and already she had noticed how big a gap there was in her life when he wasn't around.

After two years of avoiding any sort of relationship with a man she was finding that she missed the satisfaction of working with Wolff as part of the team, but most of all she missed seeing him on a daily basis—whether on duty at St Augustine's or outside the hospital.

'Get in quick or you'll drown,' he said through the open

passenger door, and as she ducked her head to slide inside she caught just a glimpse of his heart-stopping smile.

She pulled the car door shut to close out the raging elements and reached for the seat belt, drawing in her first breath of warm dry air permeated with the familiar mixture of soap and man as he started driving.

After one quick look at the way the passing streetlights highlighted the familiar features of his face she shut her eyes to savour his closeness and, in spite of the rain trickling down her face and inside her collar, she relaxed back against the seat as if she had finally found the place she wanted to be.

She was filled with a deep certainty that Wolff had found a solution to her problem but that wasn't the reason for her contentment.

For the first time since she'd heard that awful diagnosis and had realised what it meant for her future she wasn't certain that it *was* so all-important. For the first time she was wondering if the man who might have found a way around that problem might be more important than the solution he'd found.

'Here.' His husky voice drew her reluctantly out of her warmth-induced stupor and she saw the pale fabric he was offering in his outstretched hand. 'It's only a clean handkerchief but at least you could use it to dry your face.'

'Oh, thank you,' she said, touched by his thoughtfulness. 'It's all running off my hair down the back of my neck, and your seats are going to be soaked.'

Laura reached for the square of folded cloth gratefully, but her fingers brushed his and she nearly dropped the fine cotton when she felt the searing heat of his skin. It had felt almost like a shock from static electricity, and she was surprised that there hadn't been a visible spark between the two of them.

She glanced across at him to see if he had noticed, but either it was too dark to see his reaction while he was concentrating on his driving or he was much better at hiding it.

In a matter of minutes he was steering the car into a driveway and Laura suddenly noticed where he had taken her.

'This is your new place!' she exclaimed, pleased to see the house again. 'Have all the papers been signed?'

'And I've moved in,' he confirmed, apparently pleased by her enthusiasm on his behalf.

She peered through the rain streaming down the windscreen but visibility was too poor to discern any details about the place Wolff would now call home. She'd been so preoccupied the first time she'd been here that she couldn't remember much about it—just the fact that it had a warm and welcoming atmosphere.

'I hope you don't mind,' he said quietly as he took the keys out of the ignition and released his own seat belt to face her in the dimness. 'I'll take you back to your room if you'd prefer, but I wanted to have a word with you and I thought we would be less likely to be disturbed if I brought you here.'

'I don't mind,' Laura said, smiling at her understatement. It would have been more accurate if she'd said that she was delighted to be here. . .delighted to be with him. . .

'Well, then, let's make a dash for it,' he suggested, and flung his door open.

By the time Laura had followed him to the front door Wolff had unlocked it so that she could walk straight in.

He paused just long enough to aim the automatic locking device at his car before he shut the door and enclosed the two of them in his new house.

'Give me your parka and go through to the sitting room. I'll fetch a couple of towels,' he suggested.

Laura shed her wet jacket gratefully, then watched as he draped it over the newel post at the bottom of the stairs and set off up them two at a time, his long legs making short work of the distance.

Laura paused in the hallway just long enough to realise that she hadn't been mistaken about the atmosphere in the house. It felt as if each of the people who had lived here had left a little of their happiness behind in the air, and it was now settling around her shoulders like a friendly arm.

The sitting room was the one she remembered best from their inspection tour, but last time it had contained only the carpets left by the previous owners. Now it boasted curtains of a dark ivory colour and a suite of furniture framed in natural wood and upholstered in an earthy mixture of ivory and terracotta.

'What do you think?' Wolff demanded cheerfully as he held out a thick fluffy towel. 'It's gone together quite well, hasn't it?'

'It's lovely,' Laura agreed. 'I can't believe you've got it all done so quickly.'

'It's amazing how eager Leo was to help me move in,' Wolff said with his tongue firmly in his cheek.

'You mean how eager he was to help you move *out*,' she corrected with a laugh. 'I'm just surprised by how perfect it all looks.'

As she began to rub the moisture out of her hair she turned in a circle and spotted a row of low-level bookcases, filled with a mixture of well-thumbed paperbacks and more formal-looking medical tomes, a state-of-the-art hi-fi system and a richly gleaming coffee-table with the remote control for the television.

'It looks as if you've been here for ages,' she said in amazement. 'It doesn't seem possible that the whole place was empty three days ago—I didn't think anyone could move that fast.'

'I think my solicitor managed to find some short cuts,' he said vaguely. 'Anyway, I told him that, barring plans to knock it down and build a motorway straight through it, I wanted it. It's just perfect for what I need.'

'Well, I'm amazed,' she said with a shake of her head.

That reminded her that she needed to give her hair another rub. The warmth of the room had helped, but there were still chilly drips sliding off the end of each strand.

She emerged from the soft caramel-coloured towel with every hair standing on end and laughed.

'It's all right for you,' she complained as she tried to smooth the tangle into some sort of order. 'You had yours cut so short that it must just about dry by itself. I bet it was different when you had it long.'

She saw the momentary shadow cross his face as he remembered what he'd been doing when his hair had grown so long and she bit her tongue but it was too late to stop him remembering.

'Actually,' he began after she watched him deliberately pull down an invisible shutter on the memories, 'apart from the problem of keeping it free from lice, when the weather turned so cold so quickly it was very useful for keeping my head warm. I'm hoping I'll acclimatise to being shorn fairly quickly because, at the moment, I freeze every time I set foot outside!'

Laura laughed, pleased that he was able to make a joke instead of allowing the past to intrude between them.

'How about a coffee?' he offered as he relieved her of the damp towel. 'That should complete the thawing-out process.'

Laura accepted, but as she followed him through to the kitchen she sensed that he wasn't quite as relaxed as he appeared.

'Oh, I like this,' she said when he switched on the light. She didn't remember this room from their first tour but once again the colour scheme was a mixture of earth tones and natural wood, with matt ivory tiled walls and dark honey tiles on the floor. 'It looks sort of edible—a bit like *crème caramel*.'

In no time he had filled two large pottery mugs with the steaming brew and slid one across to Laura.

'Would you like a guided tour?' he offered, and she had the strange feeling that he had only suggested it as a way of procrastinating.

As she followed him out into the hallway she wondered briefly if her instincts had been wrong.

When he'd been waiting for her outside the hospital she'd been almost certain that the reason he'd been there was because he'd found a way to help her, but now. . .

Had he suggested showing her around the house to delay the moment when he would have to tell her that his idea *hadn't* worked out?

Knowing how sympathetic he'd been when she'd told him about her endometriosis, it would be quite likely that

he would be worried about how she was going to take the
bad news.

That would explain the strange air of tension which
seemed to surround him. . .

She was preoccupied when he led the way upstairs, noting almost absent-mindedly that things looked far more
sparse up here.

The bathroom was well appointed but spartan rather
than opulent, with a shower head over the bath and no
fancy extras, and the spare bedroom, which he told her
he was thinking of turning into an office or study, was
completely bare.

Then there was only one door left and Laura felt an
unexpected quiver of nervous excitement deep inside at
the prospect of seeing where he slept.

He pushed the door open silently and invited her to enter
with a graceful gesture.

Laura stepped past him, careful not to brush against him,
but even so she was aware of his eyes following her as if
he needed to see her reaction to this most personal room.

Once again there were too few possessions in the room
for it to look cluttered but, after a quick glance round, the
one thing her eyes focused on was the bed.

'A *brass* bed?' she questioned in amazement. 'That's
the *last* thing I would have expected.'

'And what *would* you have expected, always supposing
you'd given it any thought?' he asked mischievously.

Oh, Lord! she thought as she felt the start of a blush. If
he knew exactly how many times in the last week she'd
imagined his bed and. . . On second thoughts, thank goodness he *didn't* have any idea. . .

'Oh,' she said airily, hoping it sounded as if she was

making suggestions off the top of her head. 'Perhaps a king-sized modern divan, or a Japanese futon, maybe even a solid wood four-poster—not one of those modern monstrosities with curlicues and frilly curtains but a genuine heavy antique one, built to last for centuries.'

'Quite a comprehensive list, with not a brass one among them,' he agreed. 'But, then, you couldn't have known that this one was passed down to me by my grandparents with generations of stories of good luck and happiness.'

Laura looked at it with new eyes, imagining how many lives had been entwined in the history of the bed, then dragged her eyes away again before she started imagining Wolff stretched out on it, his body entwined. . .

'Well, I'm absolutely amazed at how quickly you've settled in,' she reiterated with a last look around.

'I had a few things in storage—like the bed and the suite—but my last place was a furnished rental so there wasn't very much to unpack. Just my books and a few clothes.'

'No cupboards full of exotic underwear?' she teased, remembering his reaction when she'd found the costume he *should* have been wearing that night.

'If you're talking about that wretched costume again,' he growled as he trapped her gaze with his, 'I'd like to remind you about the rather obvious effect you had on me when we were dancing. *Then* tell me if you wish I had been wearing that skimpy bit of nonsense.'

Heat blazed in Laura's cheeks as she shared the potent memory of their mutual arousal, and suddenly she couldn't look away from him.

Several times since she'd met him she'd seen that predatory look directed at her from his icy blue eyes, but never with the same intensity as this.

They weren't cold now but seared her with a laser's heat that travelled through her like a bolt of lightning.

Every cell in her body seemed to be responding to him, her heart pounding and her breathing ragged as her breasts grew tight and her most intimate places liquefied with the need to join with him.

For two years she'd avoided getting close to a man, physically or mentally, but once she'd met Wolff it was as if she didn't have a choice any more.

The old fear of being let down, being hurt the way Peter had hurt her, surfaced briefly. At a time when she'd needed support and understanding he'd thought only of himself, and it had left her afraid to trust.

But Wolff was nothing like Peter, and she wasn't even the same person she'd been then. . .

While a myriad thoughts whirled around inside her head she realised that Wolff was waiting with a predator's patience, his eyes never leaving hers as he watched the progression of thoughts leave their mark on her expression.

Like his namesake, he had a hunter's instincts and she suddenly knew that when he was this hungry he would pursue his prey relentlessly. . .

She shivered, but she knew it wasn't fear which caused all the hairs to lift on the back of her neck. It was awareness.

As they gazed deeply into each other's eyes across the width of his grandparents' bed she realised that it was time to let go of all her old fears.

Wolff desired her, a fact she'd known instinctively from the first time they'd met, and—in spite of the fact that he knew about her problems—the message in the eyes looking at her now was that he still desired her. . .more than ever.

A surge of certainty lifted her heart and she felt a smile start to curve her lips.

There were no guarantees in life and precious few second chances, but if there *was* a chance for happiness with Wolff, no matter how short-lived, she was going to grasp it with both hands.

Slowly, never taking her eyes away from his, Laura took the first step towards him, her footsteps all but silent on the soft thick pile of the carpet.

As she drew closer she grew more and more certain that she had made the right decision, and the fire in Wolff's eyes was almost incendiary when suddenly the shutters came down and he turned away from her.

Laura's steps faltered, his reaction like a physical blow.

Had she been wrong? Was it wishful thinking which had made her see desire where there was none?

'Wolff?' she said uncertainly when he didn't say anything, and he glanced briefly in her direction without meeting her eyes.

'I. . . My coffee's gone cold,' he began almost hesitantly. 'Does yours need topping up?' She nearly laughed at the prosaic comment. She'd been expecting. . .hoping for. . .a proposition, and instead she'd been offered more coffee!

With a silent nod she followed in his wake as he led the way back downstairs, still not certain whether to laugh or cry at the way things were turning out.

She'd spent so long with her emotions locked away, and the very time she'd decided to set them free. . .

She wrapped her arms around herself, chilled to the core as questions proliferated inside her head.

He'd had time to think about what she'd told him. Had

he decided that, in spite of the fact that he found her desirable, he didn't want to get involved?

She needed to think.

She needed to shut herself in her room at the hospital and replay everything that had happened this evening, analysing it until she understood what was going on.

'Wolff, I think it's time I. . .'

'Laura, about that idea I. . .'

They both came to a halt and there was silence while they each absorbed the fragments of sentences they had heard.

It was Wolff who continued.

'Please, Laura, will you stay a little longer, or would you rather I took you back?'

'You said. . .' She drew in a sharp breath as her heart began to pound again, this time with a different sort of excitement, and her words began tumbling out one over the other in their rush to be spoken.

'Oh, Wolff, have you found something out?' she demanded. 'Is there a way of getting round the system and fooling the grapevine? Have you found some way for me to remain anonymous while I try to get pregnant?'

'Hold on, Laura,' he said, a strained smile on his face as he still avoided meeting her eyes. 'It's not quite as easy as that and. . .' He stopped, blew out an exasperated sigh and gazed up at the ceiling as if for inspiration.

'Please, Wolff, I'm dying of suspense,' she begged, carefully depositing her pottery mug of coffee on the work-surface before she snatched a nervous breath and continued.

'Have you thought of some way for me to try to get pregnant without the whole hospital finding out I'm going to the fertility clinic?'

'Yes, but. . .'

'Oh, Wolff!' She flew across the short distance between them and flung her arms round him, narrowly avoiding his own mug of coffee.

'Hang on, Laura!' he exclaimed, twisting to put the hot liquid in a safer place, but he didn't break her hold, and Laura noticed that he hadn't really tried very hard.

'Tell me, please,' she begged. 'How do I avoid being seen?'

'By not going to the fertility clinic,' he said simply.

'But. . .'

'Think about it,' he continued. 'You only need to go to the fertility clinic if you are physically incapable, for one reason or another, of becoming pregnant. Right?'

'Right,' she agreed. 'But. . .'

'And so far,' he continued, ignoring her rider, 'you have no reason to suppose that the endometriosis has irreparably damaged your ovaries. In other words, because of the irregularities in your system it might take longer to achieve fertilisation, but there's actually no physical reason why you shouldn't get pregnant eventually.'

Laura nodded seriously.

'No one has ever actually put it that clearly, Wolff, but of course you're quite right.'

'So, in actual fact, the only reason why you would need to go to the fertility clinic would be to have your own egg fertilised.'

'Exactly,' she agreed, whirling away to walk to the other side of the kitchen and back, suddenly frustrated that the conversation had circled back to the same point. 'And that's why I need to go. . .'

'So, really,' he interrupted quietly, 'all you need is a willing sperm donor.'

His soft words stopped her in her tracks and she spun back to stare at him.

'You're right,' she breathed, stunned by the simplicity of it, then she froze as the implications of what he'd said dawned on her, and as her heart went crazy inside her chest she found herself examining his face very closely.

He had that expression in his eyes again, the one that made her think of a hungry wolf on the prowl, and her heart began to beat heavily against her ribs as her thoughts suddenly became very clear.

Yes, she needed a sperm donor if she was ever going to become pregnant and, logically, she didn't need to go to the fertility clinic to find one.

But while her mind was calmly listing the basic facts her heart was filled with the sudden realisation that there was only one man she wanted to be the father of her child.

A hint of uncertainty made her drag her eyes away from the heat in his.

Was he hinting that *he* would be willing to be the donor, or was that just wishful thinking on her part?

'Well?' he demanded, his deep voice huskier than ever. 'What do you think?'

She flicked a glance back at him and was surprised at the hint of vulnerability in his expression. All she had to do now was choose her words carefully so that she didn't end up embarrassing both of them.

'What are you suggesting?' she asked faintly, tempted to cross her fingers for luck.

She watched him draw in a deep breath, as though bracing himself, and his chin inched up as if in expectation of a blow.

'I could do it, if you like,' he offered steadily, and Laura began to breathe again.

'You'd be willing to donate sperm for me?' she questioned as happiness flooded through her.

She hardly noticed the way he flinched at her words, too overjoyed that it was Wolff who had shown her how to fulfil her dream and Wolff who was willing to father a child for her.

'If you like,' he agreed tersely.

Laura sighed with relief as she uncrossed her fingers and then giggled, almost as giddy as if she'd been drinking. 'Oh, yes, I like,' she said. 'Oh, Wolff, how can I ever thank you? If you only knew. . .'

'Well,' he interrupted abruptly, his clipped tone bringing her feet back down to earth in a hurry, 'where do we go from here? When do you want to start, and how well regulated is your cycle?'

Laura looked up at him, puzzled by the hint of anger in his voice. He couldn't be regretting his offer already, could he? It was a sobering thought.

'I suppose I should start as soon as possible,' she suggested sensibly. 'Bearing in mind that I don't know how fast the endometriosis is progressing.'

One of the things she remembered very clearly from the consultation with the specialist was the possibility that her form of endometriosis could eventually damage her ovaries so much that she would become totally infertile. It could be just a matter of time. . .

'As for my cycle. . .' She paused to do some mental calculations and her pulse doubled at the result. 'I should be in my most fertile phase in about a week.'

'Fine.' He nodded, the expression in his eyes hidden

behind those sinfully long lashes as though he didn't want her to know his thoughts any more.

'I know you're taking people's temperatures all day, but do you know how to chart your basal body temperature so that you can tell when you ovulate?'

This was his doctor's voice, calm and professional, and it helped her to respond the same way.

'I know that there is a slight dip in my normal temperature when the egg is actually released, and then it rises a bit above normal until the end of my cycle.'

'Is it a clear difference?'

'Yes, I'm one of the lucky ones—apart from the fact that the endometriosis means that I can almost feel the egg being released.'

'What?' He seemed quite startled.

'Yes.' She smiled wryly. 'I get quite a sharp pain at the time of ovulation—*when* it occurs—but the cycles when there is no egg released are becoming more frequent. . .'

He nodded, an expression of sympathy warming his shuttered face for a moment.

'In which case. . .'

'Where did you. . .?'

Once again they had started speaking together, and he gestured for her to continue.

'I was only going to ask where you thought we should. . . do it?' she questioned diffidently, feeling the heat rise in her face again.

'Wherever you would feel most comfortable,' he replied easily, before adding with a frown, 'except it might cause gossip if I'm seen going in and out of your room.'

'Would. . .would you mind if we did it here?' she asked

with a swift mental image of the wonderful brass bed up in his room.

'I wouldn't mind at all,' he agreed with a small smile. 'It's more peaceful here, with no nosy colleagues keeping an eye on your visitors, and, anyway, if we're successful it would be one more happy story to add to the tale of my grandparents' bed!'

Laura smothered a gasp of shock. Had he been reading her mind?

'Do you think we've covered everything?' he asked while she was still enmeshed in visions of herself lying in the middle of his family heirloom bed.

'I. . .I think so,' she stammered, scrambling for her common sense.

'In which case, I'll wait for you to tell me when the time is right,' he said, and her heart took a sudden dive when he began fishing for his keys.

'*And* hope that the two of us aren't on shifts at opposite ends of the day when the time comes,' she added wryly. 'I know of several nurses married to doctors who reckon a hospital duty roster means they don't need contraceptives—they're never home at the same time for there to be any risk that they'll get pregnant. . .'

Wolff chuckled briefly, his expression lightening a little at the typical hospital pessimism.

'Well, Nick Prince is due back this week after his honeymoon in Brittany,' he pointed out. 'That should take the pressure off *my* timetable. Do you want me to see what I can do to synchronise the two of us?'

'Don't you dare!' she squeaked, secretly delighted that he would even suggest the idea. 'Never mind the department gossiping—the whole hospital would have a field day if you did that!'

'It might be worth it,' he suggested cheekily. 'I haven't started to build up any sort of a reputation yet—apart from the rather adolescent one Leo has been trying to revive.'

'You'd certainly have a reputation if you were seen to be involved with me, and then several months later I start looking as if I've swallowed a watermelon!' she reminded him.

He grinned at her but she saw his eyes flick down to her slender waist and linger for a moment, as though he was imagining what she would look like with her body swollen with his child, and when he met her eyes again he was looking strangely thoughtful.

CHAPTER NINE

'Nurse?'

Laura looked up from the trolley. The department had been frantically busy this afternoon and she'd been left on her own in the treatment room to finish clearing away after a mammoth session of stitching up hooligans after a bottle fight outside the local football ground.

She'd been checking the level of supplies of needles and sutures when the tentative voice broke into her concentration.

'Can I help you?' she asked him with a smile. 'Are you lost?'

Automatically her eyes travelled over his pale, clammy-looking face. He could just be nervous but, patient or visitor, she didn't like the look of him.

'My chest hurts. . .and my arm. I don't feel very well. . .'

He doesn't look very well, either, she thought, and was almost certain that he was a prime candidate for a heart attack.

'Come and sit down,' she said, clearing off the top of the trolley with a speed born of adrenaline and intuition and putting a hand under his elbow to help him hitch himself up.

'In fact, you might as well lie down and be comfortable,' she suggested, supporting his shoulders as she lowered him easily on to his back. There was hardly anything of him, she thought as she reached for the phone. He hardly weighed any more than she did, and he was several inches taller—hardly the picture of a typical heart-attack victim.

Sister MacDonald answered on the second ring and Laura spared a glance at the man, lying there with his eyes shut, before she turned away to muffle her voice a little.

'A patient has just walked into treatment room two, apparently without being processed through Reception. He's pale and clammy and suffering chest pain,' she said succinctly, hoping that the man couldn't hear her speaking because he would be able to tell from her tone that she thought it was something serious.

'I've got him lying down but I'm the only one here and I need assistance,' she finished calmly.

'Good lass,' Celia said. 'Hang on and I'll send the team. He'll need the heart monitor and IVs, oxygen and blood for testing. In the meantime, start on his vital signs.'

In the absence of any case notes, Laura grabbed a drug company's promotional notepad, coincidentally advertising a tablet designed to combat high blood pressure, and began jotting down her findings.

As she spoke calmingly to him she was able to add details of the man's name and date of birth, but what she was really waiting for was the team to arrive before something major happened.

She had a nasty feeling about him.

It seemed like hours until there was the sound of hurrying feet in the corridor, and within seconds they were surrounded as the monitor leads were attached and IVs set up.

There was a brief pause when the bloods were sent up to the lab, and Laura had perched herself on a stool near the man's head to copy the details she'd scribbled down onto his new file when he made a funny sound.

She looked at his face and, if anything, he looked worse than when he'd wandered in, in spite of the oxygen mask and the two IVs.

Suddenly the rhythm of the heart monitor changed and a quick glance up at the screen showed her the horribly familiar pattern for ventricular tachycardia.

At that moment she was the closest person to the patient, and she knew that if something wasn't done fairly quickly his heartbeat could degenerate still further into ventricular fibrillation or even full cardiac arrest.

There was no time to think, no time to speak. She just leapt to her feet, vaguely aware that the sheets of paper in the carefully ordered file had just tumbled to the floor as she locked her fingers together into a double fist and thumped him in the middle of his chest.

'Good girl. You beat me to it,' said Wolff, his husky voice coming from just behind her shoulder as they both looked up at the monitor and confirmed that the sudden shock had converted his rhythm back to normal.

'You've got good reactions,' he said approvingly as he checked the man over and confirmed that his heart and breathing rhythms were back to normal again. Then he looked over at her to share a brief smile of success before it was back to business.

'Can we get that box of tricks to spit out an ECG trace as fast as possible? Then we can get him organised for a trip to the cardiologist,' Wolff said to the team, as calmly as if they hadn't just nearly lost their patient. 'He walked in here just in time on the right day, and Laura managed to react fast enough just now to keep him going. He's had a second chance and I think he deserves to get three out of three so let's get moving.'

Laura went to retrieve the scattered notes and saw a slightly nonplussed expression on the patient's face, as if everything was happening too fast for him to take it all in.

'I'm sorry I had to hit you,' she murmured apologetically. 'Are you all right?'

He smiled, his face carrying a little more colour now that the first drugs were stabilising him, and tilted his head towards Wolff.

'If he said he reckons I should get three out of three then I'd jolly well better be all right, hadn't I? Thanks for whatever it was you did just then. . .I couldn't catch my breath for a minute.'

It wasn't long before their unexpected patient was on his way upstairs, and Laura surveyed the debris left behind with a sigh before she set to again to put the room to rights.

She was on late shift today, and had been feeling rather tired and lethargic for several hours. At least tomorrow was a day off again and, noise permitting, she'd be able to catch up on some sleep.

It didn't seem possible that it was over a week since Wolff had been waiting outside the hospital and had given her a lift to his new home.

The last thing she'd been expecting when she went with him was the startling offer he'd made, and several times during the last week she'd wondered if she'd dreamt the whole thing.

But then she would catch sight of him around the department, and when he lifted one dark eyebrow in a silent question she knew that it had actually happened.

At odd times, when they were on the same shift, he seemed to deliberately take his breaks at the same time as she did, almost as if he wanted to build up some sort of rapport with the woman who was hoping to carry his child.

While she was nervous of allowing herself to become too drawn to him, she had to admit that she enjoyed his company and she'd already found out that they shared the same wry sense of humour.

The trouble was that there were too many observant eyes around them and, at some stage or another, both Leo and Hannah had spotted Wolff and herself silently communicating their opinions of events going on around them.

When the A and E consultant himself had sent them a questioning look after an unexplained simultaneous chuckle, she had blushed scarlet and wished that the ground would open up and swallow her—but she couldn't make herself regret the growing closeness she felt towards him.

'No change?' a husky voice murmured for the second time that day, and she nearly jumped out of her skin.

'You again!' she muttered, glancing around quickly to see if they could be overheard. 'I thought the arrangement was that *I* would let you know.'

'Yes, but. . .'

'But nothing,' she said fiercely. 'If we carry on this way everyone's going to wonder what's going on and, anyway, this could be an anovular cycle, and if there's no egg released my temperature *won't* change.'

'All right, all right!' Wolff held his hands up and backed off with a grin at her unaccustomed snappishness. 'Don't kill me, you might want me later.'

'I'm too tired to dig a six-foot hole,' she said darkly. 'So you're safe—for now.'

He was still chuckling as he strode away down the corridor, leaving her to her thoughts.

That was the problem in a nutshell, she complained

silently. He'd joked about the fact that she might be needing him later but, if her X-rated dreams were anything to
go by, she already needed him now—desperately.

She'd tried to rationalise her feelings, reminding herself
that he'd only offered to be a sperm donor—not a husband—but she couldn't get her stupid heart to listen.

Now every time she was near him, even when they were
in the middle of a traumatic situation, she was aware of
his presence beside her, and when his shift was over she felt
lonely, although she was surrounded by the usual throng in
the department.

Apart from the fact that Nick Prince and his new bride
were still the focus of all sorts of jokes, today was much
like any other day in the A and E department.

They could tell that the flu season was already in full
swing by the number of people turning up convinced that
they were dying—or else coughing so badly that they
wished they were.

There had been the usual mixture of time-wasters and
the genuine emergencies which sent the adrenaline pouring
into her system and kept her on her toes, but nothing
seemed to keep her mind away from Wolff Bergen for long.

Just this afternoon there had been a particularly harrow-
ing asthma attack when an eleven-year-old girl had
suddenly gone into cardiac arrest.

She'd had to be shocked before they could get her back,
but when she had finally been stabilised and sent off on
her way to the ward they'd all looked at each other with
a communal grin of success.

Suddenly Laura realised that she was beginning to feel
as if she'd been accepted as a full member of the team,

and she couldn't help the smile of delight she threw in Wolff's direction.

Finally, it was the end of her shift and she made her way gratefully towards her room.

On the chest of drawers lay the cylinder containing her thermometer and she pulled a face at it, wondering if it was worth bothering with it tonight. It looked as if this cycle was going to be one of her increasing number of anovular ones, and she was going to have to cross her fingers and wait until next month before she could make her first attempt at conceiving.

She shrugged and finally reached for it, slipping it under her tongue to 'cook' while she rummaged for a fresh towel and got ready to take a long hot shower. Perhaps then she'd feel as if she'd got a bit more energy or, if not, she could always have an early night and hope to feel better in the morning.

When the time was up she glanced disconsolately at the silvery line of mercury and prepared to shake it back down, ready for tomorrow morning, then froze and looked again.

'It's dropped!' she whispered in disbelief, and suddenly realised why she'd been feeling off-colour all afternoon. 'It's dropped!' she repeated, her hand beginning to shake so that she couldn't see the evidence any longer.

All at once her mind went blank, and she couldn't remember what she and Wolff had arranged to do when this happened.

She had to contact him. . .but how?

By telephone. . .but what was his number?

He wrote it down on a piece of paper. . .but where had she put it?

Suddenly she was racing round her room like a mad-

woman, opening and closing drawers and peering in
pockets.

'Think!' she ordered herself as she stood in the middle
of the room. 'What did you do with it when he gave it
to you?'

She closed her eyes and remembered the mock-furtive
way he'd handed her the tightly folded scrap of paper—
as if he were a desperate spy, handing over international
secrets.

'In my pocket!' she muttered triumphantly, then
remembered that it had been several days ago and the
pocket in question had been washed—probably twice
by now.

A vague picture formed in her mind of the last lot of
washing she'd sorted, and she remembered emptying several unwanted messages into the bin. Had Wolff's been
one of them?

She sank to her knees and prepared to sort through
cleanser-soaked cotton-wool and paper hankies to see if
the precious number was lurking at the bottom—but the
bin was clean and empty, and she remembered tipping all
the rubbish away when she'd cleaned her room this morning before she went on duty.

Laura stood in the middle of the room with fists planted
on her hips and groaned aloud.

What was she going to do now?

The gleam of light off her small bunch of keys drew her
eyes and, finally, her brain was working again.

She knew where he lived, and she knew that he was off
duty this evening. All she had to do was turn up on his
doorstep and apologise for coming without warning.

The thought that he might have visitors with him was

daunting but she could always offer to come back later. It wasn't as if the process was going to take very long. . .

She slid her arms back into her parka and grabbed a small carrier bag from the little stack she'd saved from her shopping trips. A quick glance inside her wash bag confirmed that the items she'd put ready were tucked into the side pocket, and she slid the whole thing into the camouflage of the plastic bag before she grabbed her keys and let herself out.

All the way over to Wolff's house she was assailed with last-minute doubts and fears.

Was she doing the right thing?

A swift mental image of herself cradling a dark-haired infant while he suckled at her breast sent a shaft of longing through her. Just the thought that it might never happen if she didn't seize the chance she'd been offered was enough to dispose of that qualm.

But was Wolff still willing. . .?

That was something she wouldn't know until she'd told him that she'd ovulated and had watched the expression on his face.

She drew her elderly Mini to a halt outside his house and saw from the thin sliver of light showing down one edge of the curtains that there was someone home.

The time for procrastination was over. Now all she had to do was to get out of the car and knock on his door.

'Laura!'

At least he sounded pleased to see her, she thought as her knees knocked like castanets.

'Come in,' he invited, standing back so that she could enter the welcoming warmth of the hallway. 'This is a surprise. What can I do for you?'

He stood there, surrounded by the smell of exotic food and looking absolutely delicious, and asked her what he could do for her? If her heart kept misbehaving the way it was he was going to have to practise cardiac resuscitation off duty.

What *had* she come here for?

'I. . .I'm sorry to just turn up like this,' she said nervously as she remembered the reason for her journey. 'But when I looked I couldn't find the piece of paper. . .with your telephone number on it. . .and. . .'

'And?' There was a gleam of patient humour in his eyes at her stumbling explanation.

'And it's gone down,' she announced baldly. 'This evening when I got back to my room I took it and it's gone down.'

She saw the second when he finally realised what she was talking about.

'You mean your temperature dipped? You've ovulated?' The expression of fierce gladness in his eyes took her breath away.

If she'd had any lingering doubts about his continued willingness to help her get pregnant they were dispelled in that instant.

'Ah, Laura, I'm so pleased for you,' he said, and drew her into his arms for a spontaneous hug. 'All week I've seen you getting more and more tense as you worried about it, but now. . .' He lifted her off her feet and swung her round in a circle until she laughed out loud.

'Wolff, you idiot! Put me down!'

'Certainly not,' he retorted, and, instead, reached down to hook one arm under her legs so that he was now carrying her in his arms as he set off towards the kitchen.

'What are you doing, you crazy man?' she demanded as he deposited her on the first chair inside the door.

'Settling you at the table before I feed you,' he announced, and reached out towards the stove to turn the heat on again.

'Feed me? But. . .'

That wasn't what she'd expected to happen when she'd come here to make her announcement.

'I haven't eaten yet, and I doubt whether you've had time to.' He raised an eyebrow in her direction and she had to shake her head.

'I was actually expecting to feed Leo tonight,' he explained. 'It was supposed to be a thank-you for putting up with my mess while I looked for this place, but he called off at the last minute. Apparently, he's swapped shifts tonight for some reason. And as I happen to have enough food prepared to feed an army you are quite welcome to share.'

He turned back towards the stove and tipped the first lot of ingredients into the wok, stirring the sizzling mixture with casual competence. Several aromatic and pungent additions later he tipped everything into the large serving bowl he'd placed to warm in the oven and carried it over with the two ready-warmed plates, a chilled bottle of white wine under his arm.

'Fork or chopsticks?' he offered with a grin, and she accepted the challenge.

'Chopsticks, on condition that I don't have to clean the floor!'

She laughed at his disgusted expression, then proceeded to show him that she was as adept at handling them as he was.

By the time they'd argued over the last of the cashew nuts and snow peas and taken the last of the wine through to the sitting room to linger over while they talked, Laura was so relaxed that she had almost forgotten why she'd come to his house.

As she drained the last sip of the deliciously crisp wine from her glass and leant back into her corner of the settee she half-heartedly offered to help with the washing up, but he shook his head.

'I'll do that in a little while,' he said quietly, his eyes suddenly intent as he met her questioning gaze, and instantly her nerves began to tighten again.

'Should I. . .? Do you. . .?' She stopped and snatched a quick breath into suddenly constricted lungs.

'Hey, Laura, relax,' he murmured and reached one hand out towards her along the back of the settee.

He combed his fingers through the silky strands of her hair and cupped her cheek, a gentle smile playing over his mouth.

'It will be all right. . .' he said softly. 'I promise. . .'

'I'm sorry, Wolff.'

She drew in a calming breath and forced herself to meet the concern in his eyes. 'I do trust you, but. . .I'm a bit nervous. I've never done this before.'

'In which case you'll be glad to hear that I've done some research on the subject,' he announced with a perfectly straight face.

'I've never heard it called that before,' Laura said, and couldn't help chuckling.

'I don't mean *that*!' he retorted, trying to sound offended. 'I actually meant that I've done some research

into the guidelines offered by the fertility clinics to maxi-
mise the chances of conception.'

'Oh,' Laura breathed, and felt the wash of heat along
her cheek-bones. 'I see.'

'Not yet, but you will!' he promised with a wicked smile.
'Now listen while I give you your instructions.'

'Yes, sir!' She gave him a mock salute.

'That's good!' he said. 'Start as you mean to go on!
Now, while I do the washing up, I want you to go upstairs
and do whatever will make you comfortable. You're welcome to have a bath or a shower and just help yourself to
anything you need.'

Laura nodded and swallowed, unable to meet his eyes
as she scrambled awkwardly out of the comfortable settee
and hurried up the stairs.

It hardly seemed as if five minutes had passed before
she heard the sound of Wolff's feet coming up the stairs
and she froze just inside his bedroom door like a frightened
deer, poised for flight.

As she'd expected she heard the click of the bathroom
door, followed by the sound of the shower running and
then silence. . .

Her cheeks grew fiery as her imagination ran riot. She'd
left everything ready for him on the shelf by the basin,
knowing that he would be bound to find it.

All she had to do while she was waiting was remember
to keep breathing—or he might just come in and find her
unconscious on the floor.

'Laura?'

She hadn't heard him leave the bathroom and the sound
of his husky voice so close behind her gave her such a
shock that she jumped visibly and whirled to face him.

'Wolff?' she whispered, her breath completely stolen away by the sight of him, all golden tan and long powerful muscles, the broad wedge of his torso covered with a scattering of damp silky hair arrowing down towards his lean waist and hips.

His towel was a much smaller version of the large one she'd borrowed to wrap around herself, and it scarcely hid the bare essentials.

For several long seconds her eyes travelled admiringly from his shoulders to his feet and back again, and she wished she'd had the courage to ask him to impregnate her the traditional way.

But he'd only offered to be a sperm donor and, instead, they'd be using the syringe she'd left ready for him in the bathroom, and she would just have to be grateful for that.

She cast one last covetous look over his broad shoulders and forced her eyes up to meet his—to discover that he was frowning.

'Is. . .is there a problem?' she asked when she finally realised that he was empty-handed.

'Yes and no,' he answered cryptically, his husky voice seeming deeper than ever as he stepped close enough for her to feel the heat radiating from his body.

'Didn't you find. . .? Couldn't you. . .?' The words wouldn't come past the lump in her throat as embarrassment overwhelmed her and she subsided into silence.

'Laura?' He hooked one warm finger under her chin and tilted her head up until she finally met his eyes. 'Do you trust me?' he asked, and she could see in his eyes that her answer mattered to him.

She nodded.

'Yes, Wolff,' she whispered, knowing that it was true.

'Then will you trust me to do my best to help you achieve your dream?'

She gazed up into his eyes, puzzled by his intensity as she tried to work out the significance of his questions.

As she searched his face for clues she watched the way his own eyes kept returning to her mouth as if it fascinated him, his pupils dilating as though just the sight of it was arousing.

Suddenly she knew what he was asking—what he wanted—and she drew her breath in on a gasp of relief and delight.

'Oh, yes, Wolff,' she said, her voice quivering with the intensity of her emotions. 'I'll trust you,' and she surged up on tiptoe to touch her lips to his.

For a second he held himself in check, as though he wasn't certain he could believe what was happening, but then his arms circled her and he covered her mouth with his, a deep groan wrenched from him as she met his marauding tongue eagerly.

Long minutes later he pulled away just far enough to allow her to catch her breath.

'Ah, Laura,' he whispered, his own breathing laboured as he gave a husky chuckle. 'If we do much more of that I'm going to have the same control problem as an adolescent, and that won't help you at all!'

He pressed one last kiss to her forehead and turned her towards his family heirloom bed.

'Let's add another chapter to the saga of the brass bed,' he invited softly, and led her across the room.

The overlap on the towel she'd wrapped around herself lasted just long enough for her to sit on the edge of the mattress before it was overcome by gravity and pooled around her waist.

'Oh!' Laura tried to retrieve it but Wolff was faster, his hand resting over hers to prevent her covering herself again.

'Let me look at you, please. You're so dainty...so beautiful.' He worshipped her with his eyes before he gave in to the temptation to touch, and once she felt his hands on her body she was lost.

As if in an enchanted dream, she followed his lead as he removed first her towel then his own and helped her to slip under the covers.

When he wrapped her in his arms it didn't feel in the least bit like the coldly clinical attempt at impregnating her that she'd been expecting, and when he explained the various theories about the best positions and optimum methods for conception to occur his husky murmur in her ear sounded far more like erotic foreplay than a scholarly dissertation.

Then he proceeded by degrees to show her all the things he'd described, with a pile of pillows underneath her hips so that they were tilted just right, before he parted her quivering thighs and joined his body with hers.

Even when his own pleasure was complete he continued to pleasure her, his hands teaching her things about her body she'd never dreamt about as he explained that her own orgasms would hasten the journey of his seed inside her.

When at last they both lay still Wolff curled around her, persuading her to stay on her throne of pillows with her legs draped over the hard support of his thighs so that she could stay comfortably in the most favourable position as long as possible.

Utterly replete, she revelled in his possessive care and

at some stage, just before she drifted off into a deliciously decadent doze, she realised with a sensation of absolute inevitability that she had fallen in love with him.

Several times during the night she was woken with kisses and gentle caresses as Wolff roused her to new heights of ecstasy, and each time she was aware that her love was growing deeper—until she had to bite her lip to prevent herself from blurting out her discovery.

The smell of coffee tantalised her and Laura lifted heavy lids to find Wolff, sitting on the edge of the bed in all his naked glory and sipping a steaming mugful as he waited for her to wake up.

'If you can spare a mouthful or two of that I might be able to focus,' Laura mumbled.

Her heart had leapt when she'd realised that he was sitting so close and for a minute she had worried what she must look like, sprawled in the tumbled wreck of his bed.

Then she realised that she didn't care if he could see more of her than she was accustomed to anyone seeing at this time of day. He had already seen and touched every inch of her during the long night, and her newly discovered love meant that she trusted him—even if he was being very mean about sharing that delicious-smelling coffee.

A slow heavy pulse began to beat deep inside her as she thought about the pleasure he'd given her through the night. They both had a day off today, and she could only imagine what delights he might initiate once she was awake enough to respond. . .

'You can have some coffee in just a minute, sleepyhead,' Wolff promised with a deep chuckle. 'First of all, open your mouth for me.'

He'd used the same words several times last night and her stomach clenched in anticipation.

Something cold and hard nudged at her lips and when she parted them in surprise she felt the familiar length of a thermometer sliding between them.

Suddenly she remembered exactly why she was lying in Wolff's bed with her hips angled up on a pile of pillows, and the effect on her was as shocking as having cold water dashed into her face.

CHAPTER TEN

AFTERWARDS, Laura could never remember what she'd said to persuade Wolff that she needed to return to her room.

The next thing she knew was that she was sitting on her bed with her arms wrapped around her waist while she rocked silently backwards and forwards.

She didn't know whether she was hoping that she *was* pregnant, so that she would always have a part of Wolff to keep with her for ever, or hoping that she *wasn't*, so that she could legitimately spend another ecstatic night in his big brass bed.

Either way, she felt emotionally shredded that, while she had fallen in love with him and had believed that they were beginning to form a deep and lasting bond, he had never lost sight of the fact that she was only in his bed so that he could help her to become pregnant.

For ten days she wondered and worried while she worked her shifts alongside him, trying to treat him as though he meant no more to her than Leo or Nick.

She knew that he had noticed the difference in her attitude towards him, and where once she would have welcomed any chance to spend time with him now she actively avoided him. It hurt too much to spend time with him, knowing that the love she felt for him was not returned.

Sometimes she felt his eyes on her, their laser intensity

almost burning, and she'd seen that terrible empty look return to their icy blue depths.

'Laura?' Hannah began tentatively when it was their turn for a coffee-break. 'Is something the matter?'

'Not that I know of,' Laura replied defensively, while the persistent little voice inside her cried out about broken hearts and broken dreams.

'I wondered if you were sorry you moved to St Augustine's after all. You don't seem to be very happy. Did. . .?' She paused, as though uncertain whether to ask the question on her tongue, then continued, 'Did you and Wolff have some sort of bust-up?'

'Wolff and I?' Laura did her best to sound amazed and amused, and apparently pulled it off.

'Well, you did seem to be getting on rather well when he first came here, and I began to wonder if there was the possibility of something developing between you. . . But then, suddenly, you were hardly speaking to each other and Wolff was growling at everyone.'

'Oh.' Laura's brain whirled as she tried to come up with an explanation, then decided to stick as close to the truth as possible. 'He did a bit of research for me several weeks ago. . .about endometriosis. But that's all there was between us.' Apart from the most fantastic night of love-making she would ever know in her life, but that was something she wasn't ever going to confide to anyone else—whether it had resulted in a pregnancy or not.

'Endometriosis?' Hannah questioned, and then she nodded as if that explained something she'd wondered about. 'I remember you having problems sometimes when we were training. Is that what it was?'

Feeling guilty about being unable to confide the details

of her arrangement with Wolff, Laura compromised by telling her about the demise of her relationship with Peter.

'Luckily, once I transferred to A and E we didn't work too closely together so I just gritted my teeth and got on with the job.' And cried private tears about all the lost dreams.

'So how soon after did he marry her?' Hannah asked with quiet understanding in her tone.

Laura gave a wry laugh. 'I couldn't help myself following what was happening, and I was bracing myself for the big event to happen fairly quickly but it didn't.'

She shook her head, knowing that the old hurts were clear in her voice but suddenly needing the catharsis.

'I thought that perhaps she wasn't too willing to give up a good career to be a brood mare, and I even found myself fantasising that he was delaying committing himself to her because he was regretting breaking up with me. . . But then, a couple of months ago, everything went ahead with a big splash.' She drew an unsteady breath.

'It was only when the grapevine dissected the reasons for the sudden rush to the altar that I found out his new bride was nearly three months pregnant—he'd obviously taken the precaution of making sure she could give him the children he wants.'

'What a rat!' Hannah said with more venom than Laura would have expected, and suddenly she realised that Hannah had her secrets, too.

Something similar must have happened to *her* in the time since they'd last been together.

She vaguely remembered that her friend had been seeing a specialist about something. . .

'If there's anything I can do you know I'm always will-

ing,' Hannah offered, her voice banishing Laura's attempt
at remembering.

'Unfortunately, some things can't be mended with a hug
or some superglue,' Laura murmured, returning to her own
concerns. 'And we can't always have our dreams, no matter
how much we want them.'

'Too true,' her friend agreed with a touch of bitterness
in her usually cheerful voice. 'Very few of us get a second
chance at happiness.'

There was the sound of approaching footsteps and Laura
recognised Wolff's voice among the others.

'Well,' she said, rising briskly to her feet, 'time I was
back at work.'

Before Hannah could utter a word she had tipped the
last of her coffee down the sink and rinsed her mug.

By the time the small knot of people had entered the
room she was already waiting to leave, her eyes carefully
averted so that she couldn't possibly catch Wolff's eye.

She knew how cowardly it was to run from the situation,
but until she knew the results of the night they'd spent
together she couldn't bear spending time with him. It tore
at her heart to know that while she had been falling more
and more deeply in love with him he had merely been
performing a biological function.

Not that she could blame him. After all, that was all he
had offered and, having listened while he'd talked about
the tragic things he had seen at the refugee camp, she could
understand that he was unconvinced about the worth of a
committed relationship.

In spite of her attempt at avoiding him, she looked up
at just the wrong time as she went to leave the room and
met his eyes full-on for the first time in over a week.

Her heart gave a sick jolt when she realised that he didn't look any happier than she felt, his eyes empty of expression, and she could have wept when she had to restrain her automatic action to reach out and comfort him.

As she dragged her eyes away and continued on her way she sternly reminded herself that she had no right to touch him, no right—other than as a fellow human being—to care that he was unhappy and wonder why.

She tapped on the door and started to walk into Sister's office before she suddenly realised that it was already occupied by a totally oblivious couple.

'Sorry,' she muttered, full of embarrassment, and smartly reversed direction.

'Don't go,' called Polly as she disentangled herself from her husband's arms. 'We're the ones who should apologise—it was totally unprofessional to be caught like that.'

'At least we're married,' her husband pointed out in their defence. 'And it was a one-off thing.'

'I hope not,' Polly muttered swiftly, then went red when she realised that she'd said the words out loud.

'What I meant,' Nick continued smoothly, to spare her blushes, 'was that the kiss was a celebration of a special event and not a habit we'll be indulging in while we're on duty.'

Laura tried not to look curious, but realised that she'd obviously failed when Polly laughed.

'If I tell you can you keep it quiet for a little while so we have time to savour it before it gets on the grapevine?'

'You don't have to. . .' Laura began awkwardly, feeling that she was intruding on something intensely private.

'I'm pregnant,' Polly blurted, and smiled lovingly up at

the big man, hovering protectively over her. 'I've just had official confirmation.'

For a second envy made the smile freeze on her face, but then the natural joy at their happiness took over.

'Congratulations. I don't need to ask if you're pleased.'

'Ecstatic,' Polly confirmed with a giggle.

'Whether she'll still feel the same when it comes to early morning feeds and changing nappies remains to be seen,' Nick warned, but it was obvious that he was just as delighted as she was.

The touching scene played on her mind all day, and the more she thought about it the more she realised that the situation between Wolff and herself couldn't go on like this.

She didn't want to leave her job, not now that she'd been accepted as a valuable member of the team and especially with the excellent career prospects ahead of her. On the other hand, knowing that Wolff had just bought a house, she knew that he would be very unwilling to move again so soon.

They were two intelligent adults, for heaven's sake. There must be some way of sitting down and thrashing out their differences or it would sour things for everyone.

A little quiver of apprehension settled deep inside her when she thought about confronting Wolff, but she promised herself that she *would* do it—just as soon as she found out whether she was pregnant or not.

She didn't have to tell him that she'd fallen in love with him, she reminded herself as she detoured into a chemist's shop on her way back to her room and stood, contemplating a display of pregnancy indicator kits. And at least once she had a result she'd have a reason to approach him to initiate the conversation.

She made her choice and cursed silently at the stupidity of a qualified nurse who at work dealt calmly and efficiently with every intimacy inside and outside the human body at work yet blushed betroot-red over buying a pregnancy test kit.

There were new road-works creating havoc on her way back to the nurses' accommodation, and she had to take the long way round before she could park her scruffy little car and scurry through the dark into the light and warmth of her room.

There had been headlights following her before she'd stopped, and when the car had drawn past her she'd imagined that it had been the one Wolff had given her a lift in when. . .

'Stop it,' she hissed into the silence of her room as she kicked off her shoes and hung her parka on the back of the door.

It was time to concentrate on reading the instructions on the packet and carrying them out. *Then* would come the time for seeking Wolff out and. . .

'Bother!' she muttered as the leaflet slid out of her fingers and fell neatly down the back of her chest of drawers. 'How am I going to get *that* out?'

She dropped to her knees in the space between the cupboard and the door of her room and tried to wriggle her fingers into the narrow gap to fish it out, but before she had any success there was an enormous roar and the sound of shattering glass as the lights went out and she was plunged into darkness.

The first thing she noticed when the noise ended was

that she was cold, then she realised that there was a heavy weight pinning her down and that it was difficult for her to draw in a breath.

The unearthly silence which had followed the roar was now filled with screams and further crashes, as well as the sound of water cascading somewhere nearby. In the distance there was the familiar reassuring sound of the siren on an approaching vehicle.

'Laura!'

She peered into the darkness, certain that she'd heard someone shouting her name, but with all the noise going on around her she could easily have been mistaken. She knew to her cost that wishful thinking could have you believing all sorts of things. . .

'Laura!'

The voice was coming closer, and this time she could hear that it *was* calling her name. She tried to call back but couldn't draw in a deep enough breath. It felt as if she had half the building sitting on her chest.

'Laura!'

The voice was right outside her room now, and if it hadn't been for the fear distorting it she would have sworn it was Wolff's voice.

'Oh, God! Please, not Laura. . .not Laura!' the voice begged, and the familiar husky tone told her that it *was* Wolff outside her door.

'Wolff. . .' she tried to call, but it emerged as nothing more than a whisper and the effort made her cough.

'Laura?' He must have heard the choking sound she made because the word was a demand this time. 'Can you hear me, Laura?'

'Yes,' she breathed on a shallow sigh, but he heard her.

'Oh, thank you, God,' she heard him mutter before there was the sound of crashes and bangs not far from her head.

Outside, too, there was a cacophony as the emergency teams began to get to grips with the situation. There was the sound of a powerful generator starting up and a bright light suddenly flooded her room as floodlights were switched on around the scene.

'Laura?' Wolff called to her again, his voice sounding as if it was just inches away from her head. 'Are you hurt?'

Laura experimentally tensed the muscles in each of her limbs but, apart from the cupboard pinning her against the wall, she seemed to be all right.

'Trapped,' she muttered succinctly with her limited air supply.

'Trapped?' he repeated.

'Yess.'

'By masonry?' he demanded, but she didn't bother making the effort to reply. He'd never have heard the soft breathy sound of the word 'no' over the sounds of rescue.

'Furniture?' he guessed, and she hissed briefly in agreement.

'Are you near the door?' he asked, and she could hear from the forced patience of his questions that he wasn't nearly as calm as he was pretending to be.

'Yess,' she whispered again, the effort quite exhausting her as she dragged the next breath in.

'If I try to open the door will I injure you more?' Wolff demanded, his patience obviously wearing very thin.

Laura turned her head this way and that while she tried to judge how firmly the furniture was wedged into the corner.

Now that there was light coming in from outside she could see that there must have been some sort of explosion

because nearly half of the outside wall had been blown
into her room, the glass from her window glittering in
deadly shards as far as she could see.

Exploring with the hand not trapped, she worked out
that if she could. . .

'Laura? Are you still with me?' The anxiety in his voice
dragged her out of her musings.

'Yess,' she answered, a tired smile creeping over her
face when she realised that he was worried about her.
It wasn't the same as loving her, but at least she knew
he cared.

'I'm going to try to open the door,' he announced, his
endurance obviously at an end. 'I'll go slowly so if you
need me to stop just hiss. OK?'

'Yess,' she agreed, her heart lifting at the thought of
release.

She heard the door catch release and braced her hand
against the heavy piece of furniture pinning her down.
Hopefully, when he started to push against it the angle at
which it had landed would allow it to slide just far enough
up the door to relieve the pressure on her ribs.

She heard his involuntary groan as he put his weight
against the door and slowly, slowly, watched the deep score
being gouged in the wood as he forced it to slide up.

By degrees the weight on her ribs eased until at last she
was able to draw her first normal breath.

'Wolff?' she called, the residual ache in her chest still
restricting the volume of her voice.

'Yes?' The grinding sounds stopped as he paused to
listen.

'If you can get your hand round the edge of the door,
about a foot from the floor, you could grab the cupboard.'

There was a brief shuffling sound on the other side of the door and she could imagine him altering his position against it so that he could reach in through the gap he'd created.

She watched the shadowy corner and saw his hand appear. It took only seconds for him to locate the edge of the chest of drawers and, although the restricted access through the narrow gap must have made it almost impossible, she watched his tendons tighten as he began to lift.

Once it had started moving momentum worked in his favour, and within seconds he had heaved the obstruction far enough to get his other hand through to help.

'Wait,' she called, and he stopped pushing instantly.

'What's the matter?' he demanded through teeth gritted with effort.

'I'm in the way. . .' She clenched her teeth and forced herself to roll over carefully so that the door could swing open. 'It's clear now,' she confirmed, and she saw the cupboard rock back onto its base when Wolff gave one last heave.

'Laura? Where are you?'

He swung the door open slowly so that he didn't hit her and stepped into the devastated room, his feet crunching on a mixture of glass and masonry as he came into view.

'Down here, catching my breath,' she panted, conscious that she was aching all over.

He crouched down beside her, one hand reaching out tentatively towards her face as though he couldn't quite believe that she was there.

'Ah, Laura, I thought I'd lost you,' he said gruffly, and cradled her cheek in his trembling palm.

Laura gazed up at him in amazement, hardly able to believe what she was hearing.

'Hey! Wolff? What are you doing here?' demanded Leo's voice, and the two of them looked up to see the first of the rescuers, working their way along the corridor, the reflective bands on their emergency uniforms ghostly in the strange light.

'You're not supposed to be in here,' Leo pointed out sternly. 'It's rescue personnel only until they tell you it's safe to come in.'

'I was already in,' Wolff told him shortly. 'I was in the stairwell on my way up when it happened. What the hell caused it? It sounded like a bomb.'

'Gas main blew,' Leo said succinctly as he focused a torch on Laura's face. 'How are you doing?' he demanded, his voice as gentle as his hands as he quickly examined her. 'Fingers and toes all in working order?'

'Apart from feeling as if I've been run over by a steam-roller, I feel fine,' she confirmed.

'In that case, we'll just get you over to A and E for a quick checkover,' he decided. 'Your room seemed to take the brunt of the explosion, and if you come out of it with nothing more than a few bruises then we've come off very lightly. Nobody lower down in the building got any more than shock and cuts from flying glass, and you were the only one up here on this side of the building.'

Wolff had stayed in the background while his friend did his job.

As the St Augustine's Hospital emergency team doctor, Leo had been trained to cope with such emergencies, and even though Wolff had probably had more experience of such situations in the last three months than Leo had had in a couple of years there was still the matter of professional courtesy.

Finally Laura was loaded onto a stretcher, her neck protected in case she'd injured it without realising it.

'It doesn't feel right, being the patient. I feel so helpless,' she mumbled, and Wolff smiled briefly, his face still showing signs of strain as he accompanied her out to the ambulance waiting to transport her.

'You don't have to stay with me,' she said, trying to be brave. 'If they need you to take care of other injured people. . .'

'I'm concentrating on one patient at a time,' he growled, and tightened his hand around hers. 'And when you've got the all-clear I'm taking you home where I can keep an eye on you!'

Wolff's husky voice made it sound like a threat but it was music to her ears.

He drove his car behind the ambulance to the emergency entrance and waited more or less patiently while her neck was X-rayed and declared clear. Then he wheeled her out of the department as if she were made of spun glass and settled her in the passenger seat.

As he drove silently out of the hospital grounds she caught a quick glimpse of the damaged corner of the nurses' accommodation and, remembering the glitter of all that glass, suddenly realised just how lucky she'd been. If she hadn't been trying to fish the instruction sheet for the pregnancy test out from behind the chest of drawers. . .

The memory flooded over her and her hand crept over to lie protectively across her stomach. She hadn't even had time to take the test so she still didn't know whether she was carrying Wolff's baby or not.

The X-ray department had made certain that her lower body was safely covered by a leaded shield before they'd taken their pictures, but that was a routine precaution they would have taken for any woman of child-bearing age. . .

Her scattered thoughts ground to a halt when Wolff drew up outside his house.

'I'm sorry,' he said gruffly into the sudden silence, 'I seem to have kidnapped you without giving you a choice as to whether you wanted to come here.'

'I want to be here,' Laura confirmed, her heart racing at the thought that he'd wanted to take her to his home, 'but I haven't got anything with me—no wash kit or clothes. Nothing.'

'You can worry about that in the morning,' he said as he released her seat belt for her and then went round to help her out of the car.

She hardly had time to swing round and put her shoeless feet out before he'd scooped her up into his arms and was carrying her up the path.

'Wolff! You'll hurt your back!' she warned with a soft laugh, hanging onto his neck with both arms as he juggled with the front door lock and took her inside.

The door swung closed behind them but he made no effort to switch on the light as he leant back against the door and held her cradled in his arms, the tension in his body overwhelming.

She could feel the way his heart was pounding against his ribs, his breathing ragged against her cheek, and she started to worry about him. He'd hardly said a word since she'd been rescued. . .

'Wolff. . .' In spite of the darkness surrounding them, she cupped his cheek unerringly with her hand and found that the skin was wet although it hadn't been raining tonight.

'Wolff, are you all right?' she demanded softly, wishing that she could see his expression. Were they tears on his face? Was he crying and, if so, why?

'Oh, sweetheart, I thought I'd lost everything,' he said hoarsely into the darkness, his voice sounding raw as he slanted his head over hers and rubbed his cheek softly over her hair. 'When I realised that there'd been an explosion and you could be injured—even dead—I couldn't bear it. . .'

He drew her closer against his chest, as if he couldn't bear to have any distance between them, and she tightened her arms around his neck—utterly content for the first time in days.

'As I ran up the stairs,' he continued, his voice sounding almost rusty, 'all I could think of was that I'd never told you that I love you and that it might be too late.'

'Oh, Wolff,' she breathed as happiness bloomed inside her. 'And all I could think of as I was lying trapped under that chest of drawers was that I couldn't breathe and that if I died I'd never have the chance to tell you that I love you.'

She felt the impact of her words as he froze.

'You love me?' he questioned, open disbelief in his tone. 'But you've hardly looked at me since we spent that night together, let alone spoken to me. I thought you'd only wanted me to make you pregnant.'

'I know,' she admitted guiltily. 'And I'm sorry if I hurt you but. . .I was in love with you and I was afraid that I might say something.'

'What? That's crazy!'

Suddenly he strode across the empty hallway and into

the sitting room, his elbow finding the light switch and flooding the room with brightness.

'Sit there,' he ordered, plonking her down on one end of the settee and marching across to shut the curtains.

Laura was quite giddy with the sudden change of pace. One minute they were standing quietly in the darkness of the hallway while they murmured loving words to each other and the next he was dumping her on the settee as if he was angry with her.

'You were in love with me and you didn't want me to know? What sort of idiocy is that?' he challenged as he sat down with his knees touching hers.

'You told me about your time in the refugee camp and you said you didn't think that relationships had a chance. You'd seen the pain and heartbreak and you didn't believe in second chances.'

'That was *then*,' he said indignantly. 'This is now— and us.'

'And that makes it different?' she queried hesitantly.

'Yes! Of course it does!' He caught her hands and wrapped them in his, bringing them up one at a time for a tender kiss.

'Then why didn't *you* tell *me*?' she demanded softly. 'Out in the hallway you said you love me, but why didn't you say it before?'

'I was going to,' he said with a wry smile on his face as he tightened his fingers around hers. 'That's why I was on my way up the stairs when the gas main blew—I couldn't bear the waiting any longer.'

'The waiting?'

'To find out if my gamble had worked—to find out if you were pregnant,' he explained. 'I've spent ten miserable days not knowing whether I wanted you *not* to be pregnant so I could persuade you to share my bed again—and maybe persuade you to fall in love with me—or whether I wanted you to be pregnant so that I could try for the gratitude vote.'

'The gratitude vote? Vote for what?'

'Marriage, of course,' he said, as if it was obvious. 'That's what I've wanted ever since you stepped up on that stage, your eyes spitting fire at me for daring to embarrass you.'

'Actually, it was fear, not fire,' she said with a smile. 'After two years without a problem I hardly had to look at you and my hormones went into overdrive. . .'

He smiled at her with a wolfish gleam in his eyes.

There was just one shadow lingering in a corner of her mind.

'Wolff, I still don't know the result,' she murmured softly, determined that there would be no secrets.

'Result?' he queried distractedly, his eyes intent on her mouth.

'Of the pregnancy test,' she explained. 'I still don't know if we managed to. . .'

'Laura, it isn't the baby I want—it's you. I love *you*, and any children we have will just be a special bonus.'

Laura heard the words and knew that he meant every one of them. Was this the man who didn't believe in second chances? Ever since she'd met him he'd been taking chances—with his heart, with her love. . .

'Anyway, it doesn't matter,' he said confidently. 'We've got plenty of time for second chances now. If we didn't manage it last time I'm sure you won't mind trying again. . .and again. . .'

'And again,' she echoed with laughter in her voice as he swept her up in his arms and made his way towards the stairs.

* * * * * * * *

Leo and Hannah have their own wonderful story in
THIRD TIME LUCKY
Look out for the final part of the trilogy
in January 1998

MILLS & BOON®

Medical Romance™

Dear Santa,

Please make this a special Christmas for us.
This Christmas we would like...

A VERY SPECIAL NEED by Caroline Anderson
'Daddy do you think you'll ever find another mummy
for me? I think I'd like to have a mummy,' Alice asked.

A HEALING SEASON by Jessica Matthews
Libby's children loved having Dr Caldwell around at
Christmas, but then it wasn't just the children who
liked him.

MERRY CHRISTMAS, DOCTOR DEAR by Elisabeth Scott
Colin told his Uncle Matt that you couldn't always be
sure what you got for Christmas, you just had to wait
and see, but they felt sure that this Christmas would be
worth waiting for.

A FATHER FOR CHRISTMAS by Meredith Webber
Richard tries hard to put his feelings for Margaret's
children down to a lack of sleep, but he isn't fooling
anybody, not least of all himself!

Christmas is for kids

...a family.
Thank you very much
The Children

Four books written by four authors from around
the world with one wish for Christmas.

Jennifer
BLAKE

GARDEN
of
SCANDAL

She wants her life back...

Branded a murderer, Laurel Bancroft has
been a recluse for years. Now she wants her
life back—but someone in her past will do
anything to ensure the truth stays buried.

*"Blake's style is as steamy as a still July
night...as overwhelmingly hot as Cajun spice."*
— Chicago Tribune

**AVAILABLE IN PAPERBACK
FROM NOVEMBER 1997**

GET TO KNOW

THE BEST OF ENEMIES

the latest blockbuster from TAYLOR SMITH

Who would you trust with your life? Think again.

Linked to a terrorist bombing, a young student goes missing. One woman believes in the girl's innocence and is determined to find her before she is silenced. Leya Nash has to decide—quickly—who to trust. The wrong choice could be fatal.

Valid only in the UK & Ireland against purchases made in retail outlets and not in conjunction with any Reader Service or other offer.